The Woods

Jack N. Lawson

A Wings ePress, Inc.
Fiction/Humor Novel

Wings Press, Inc.

Wings ePress, Inc.

Edited by: Jeanne Smith
Copy Edited by: Brian Hatfield
Executive Editor: Jeanne Smith
Cover Artist: George Lawson

All rights reserved

Wings ePress Books
www.wingsepress.com

Copyright © 2021 by: Jack N. Lawson
ISBN-13: 978-1-61309-525-6

Published In the United States Of America

Wings ePress Inc.
3000 N. Rock Road
Newton, KS 67114

The Woods

Written, apparently, in a spirit of wicked fun, this novelette debunks conventional notions of how upscale retirees behave once freed from the demands of family and career. As it turns out, at least in this writer's telling, when the elderly have no one but each other holding them to account, they become what they perhaps always were—often to hilarious or horrific effect.

The story takes place entirely at The Woods, a retirement community in central North Carolina. Each resident profiled in the tale seems defined by some ruling passion, be it a political or philosophical bent, a lifelong but never-fulfilled aspiration, an obsession perhaps heightened by dementia, or raw sexual desire.

Skewered notions of the ways elderly people deal with death litter the landscape of this story. When the children of a retired French teacher nicknamed Keska Saye present her with a Colonel Sanders bag containing the ashes of their late father, his widow contemplates what's left of a man who had committed multiple infidelities.

"'Well, Mark, there you are—Remember that blowjob I promised you?' And with that. Keska blew at the ashes, sending a plume over all four of them."

This hilarious episode hints at the dark underside to The Woods' residents' refusal to treat death with any sentiment other than scoffing dismissal. Elsewhere, that underside turns more stark, even ghoulish, and the reader's amusement might veer toward unease.

Jimmy T, the student chaplain, turns out to be this narrative's closest approach to a protagonist. He undergoes a profound change in his perspective on life at The Woods, and on life in general.

At the end of this short novel, the reader might feel torn between the seemingly simple story and its darker implications of the tendency of human beings at any stage of life to divide along lines of in-ness and out-ness, often to deadly effect.

Lawson ends his story by expanding slightly on the half-invitation, half-warning in his opening paragraph. Like Hansel and Gretel, Snow White and the Big, Bad Wolf, his characters also had all their adventures in the forest.

"Woods can conceal as well as reveal. There is mystery and beauty. At night, they harbor fear and anxiety for timid humanity, too used to artificial light. In daylight, they beckon us for a welcome stroll. Won't you come in?

—Michael Jennings, author of Ave Antonina
and Like a Wary Blessing

I've known Jack Lawson for forty years. To spend time with him is to watch his towering intellect, his soulful altruism and his wicked-dark sense of humor spar endlessly with each other. Sometimes it's inspiring. Sometimes it's challenging. And sometimes it's just twisted fun. Welcome to his novel The Woods.

—Jim Borgman, Pulitzer Prize-winning editorial cartoonist
And co-creator of the comic strip Zits

Dedication

For John H. Gardner
With gratitude, for being the sort of reader
who makes writing a true pleasure.

***

One

The Woods

Woods and forests are funny things. They hold such power over and within the human psyche. Hansel and Gretel, Snow White, the Big Bad Wolf, Robin Hood, as well as a host of others, all had their adventures in the forest—and in our imaginations. Woods can conceal as well as reveal. There is mystery and beauty. At night, they harbor fear and anxiety for timid humanity, too used to artificial light. In daylight, they beckon us for a welcome stroll.

Der Platoniker was musing over these exact things as he walked toward the dining hall. Since he first moved into The Woods, Der Platoniker had been urged by the staff to take long, leisurely walks among the trees. "It will increase your well-being and free your spirit," he was told with benign smiles.

Ah, but wait, you're wondering why an individual would bear a German moniker which utilized the definite article 'der' or 'the.' I can see why you would be puzzled. Der Platoniker means 'the Platonist,' for reasons that will become clear. But please bear with me, for other matters will become somewhat more obscured by mystery in The Woods.

As I was saying, Der Platoniker was walking through the woods which separated his little cottage, as well as the other apartments and homes, from the central building in the grounds of Carolina Woods, a retirement community set in the woods of central North Carolina. This main building contained the dining rooms, lounge, library, post office, and more. Outside the building and facing the entrance to the community stood a large wooden sign, which proclaimed:

Carolina Woods
Where You Live Your Dreams

The community was positively brimming with academic degrees, as this was a mecca for retired professors from the many nearby universities. Der Platoniker was a retired philosopher, but such description—retired—bears deeper scrutiny as one wonders whether a philosopher can ever really stop philosophizing. And Der Platoniker could never do that. He only stopped for two things: eating and sleeping. Oh, I know what you're thinking—what about bodily functions? Well, only consider what Schopenhauer had to say about food intake: *Man ist was er isst.* So you see, even a good bowel movement could be subject to critical thinking. It is a sobering fact, after all, that the by-product of every human being is shit.

All right then, there was Der Platoniker's odd dabble into the late-night German porno channel, at which he was as amused as he was aroused. After all, *Brustwart* for nipple?! How erotic sounding is that? And he chuckled as the sexual partners climaxed, shouting "*Ich spritze!*" He even found himself saying it out loud from time to time, as the onomatopoeic sound was simply amusing to him. He caught another resident looking at him curiously one day as he checked his mailbox, muttering "*Ich spritze*" under his breath. But he had only smiled nervously and left hurriedly, hoping the hearer wasn't fluent in German.

Der Platoniker's musing over the woods in which he and the several hundred other residents lived were all part of the many phenomena which both made up life and made life interesting. There were cute, meandering paths among the pines and various hardwoods. And although they were largely tamed by human hands, they still carried the air of a primeval mystique. Der Platoniker wondered: did the trees themselves hold memory within them? Did they have a collective memory or thoughts? Yes, some of the residents thought he was mad, but as a phenomenologist, all phenomena were grist for the grinding of his brain. *And there was something about these woods.*

Before becoming *Der* Platoniker, he had generally been known as Professor Reiner Gessler, tenured at a small liberal arts college in the Sandhills of North Carolina. Now, blissfully, there were no more papers to mark or over-grown adolescents to mollycoddle. Rather, he could revel in the life of the mind along with similarly gifted individuals. If you were to ask him how he got his nickname, "Der Platoniker," or even whether he minded it, he would shrug and say it just seemed to fit. As time went on, he really couldn't remember having been called anything else.

But such was the case for all residents in Carolina Woods. Take, for instance, Mach Schnell—formerly Machiavelli Schnell. Unsurprisingly he came from Italian-German parentage. His parents had been intellectuals who purportedly had fled Europe in the face of Nazi aggression. Both had been political scientists, which should provide a hint at Mach's forename. And like his surname, he was seemingly always in a hurry. So it was when Der Platoniker saw him making a bee-line for the dining room.

"Mach!" called Der Platoniker, "*Wie geht's?*" As fellow academics with German backgrounds, they often spoke in German.

"*Es geht mir gut,*" and then, as an afterthought, "*Und Ihnen?*" Mach never used the familiar '*du*' or '*dir*' with fellow residents.

"It's Saturday," called Der Platoniker, following in Mach's wake.

"Just like every week. Zo kind of you to notees," came the retort from Mach.

"No. I mean, it's time for Saturday dinner. Our weekly 'surprise.'"

"We shall see, zen, shan't we?" was all Mach had to say about it. Der Platoniker was fascinated by the fact that, although Mach had been born in the United States, he had begun to develop a German accent with the passage of time.

One thing could be said about the cuisine at Carolina Woods—it was international, which suited this global community of academics. 'Saturday Surprise' was always a take on an otherwise well-known dish: spaghetti carbonara, pulled pork barbecue, ravioli, Wiener Wurst, Thai chicken curry—you name it.

Upon arriving in the main building, Der Platoniker had the habit of checking his mail box first. He flitted through the assorted adverts and bills, then placed them all in his jacket pocket and made his way to the serving area where he would hang up his coat, as was his custom, in the passageway outside the dining hall. This was also a risky venture as the residents were very fuzzy about what belonged to whom. He was still keeping an eye out for a favorite tweed jacket which had walked away just after he had moved in. His only hope was that it had not been used to dress someone for a funeral. Next, Der Platoniker approached the serving areas.

"What's in store for us tonight?" Der Platoniker asked one of the newer servers.

"The stuff that dreams are made of," smiled the server. "It's Saturday Surprise! You'll like it. Y'all always do. Want some vegetables with that?" Der Platoniker nodded and took all that was on offer.

Der Platoniker searched the tables for friendly faces. Despite having spent his entire life alone, he preferred company when eating. He caught the eye of the retired professor of 19th century French literature, Keska Saye. The lady was always magnificently coiffed and wore scarves which accented her fully grey hair. She had met her American husband at the Sorbonne when he was a graduate student, and then moved back to the U.S. with him. They had both found teaching positions in North Carolina universities. She had recently lost her husband, but was amazingly phlegmatic about it. "Ah, dear Plato!" Her long fingers beckoned him over. She insisted on taking his name as

Plato, and was the only person Der Platoniker allowed to bastardize his name.

Keska Saye had been at The Woods, as the residents fondly called their home, for several years, and was well-established. Only newcomers, who had at least a smattering of French would, upon first hearing her pronounce her name, stammer, *"Qu'est-ce que c'est?"* confusedly, while wondering "What is *what?*" This simple *faux pas* was always overlooked by Keska, who, as you might have guessed by now, was originally called something like Veronique Labat. She too had come to forget about those days and found joyous surrender to her persona at The Woods; so Keska Saye she was, and would remain.

Keska was sitting with a married couple, Schwanzie and Twilight. Schwanzie had been a rather strait-laced professor of economics at a New York university, and had been known as Aaron Weisman—until he arrived at The Woods. Der Platoniker knew, for a fact, that Schwanzie's nickname came, first of all, from his male appendage, which was of greater proportion to his five-foot-eight frame than his other appendages. Der Platoniker had seen it for himself when using the changing rooms for the community's swimming pool. In addition, the nickname seemed also to be founded upon the many rumors floating around The Woods regarding the use to which Schwanzie put his enormous attribute within the retirement community. But of that, Der Platoniker had no direct knowledge. Although many of the widows and neglected wives did seem to sparkle whenever they saw Schwanzie. As for Twilight, she had come by her Woods name because of her fading memory and the fact that she always fell asleep at twilight. Even at concerts, cocktail parties, and special occasions, Twilight's head would be seen dropping with the sun, even when standing! She seemed blissfully unbothered by her husband's Woods-name. She was always pleasant to Schwanzie and to all of her fellow residents, for that matter. Twilight's dress sense unintentionally brought amusement to her fellow residents: mismatched shoes, underwear worn on the outside of her clothes, etc. On this particular evening, she was wearing a navy-blue cardigan, but with the button-side on her back—completely buttoned up.

'So Platoniker," began Schwanzie, "be glad you don't have children. *Nu*, our son, Herschel and his wife came to visit yesterday. And my son, the big-shot lawyer and his mousy little wife...um, Twilight dear, what, what's the name of Herschel's wife?"

"Mousy?"

"Thanks, sweetheart," Herschel raised his eyebrows at Der Platoniker over his wife's memory. "Anyway, Herschel and Mousy—ha, that'll do!—tell Twilight and me that they're worried about the standard of care here at The Woods. They think we all need dementia care! And get this, they think our Woods-names are demeaning! Can you believe that? Herschel says to me, 'Dad, don't you find it embarrassing to be called a *schmeckle?*' So I told him, I'm not called a *schmeckle,* I'm called Schwanzie—there's a difference!' So I reach over and grab my son by the crotch and say, 'This is a *schmeckle.*' Then I stand up, open my zipper and say, 'Voilà. *This* is why they call me Schwanzie.'"

Twilight giggled like a schoolgirl and said, "He did! That's just what he did!"

"Oh, I should like to have been there," gasped Keska.

"So what happened," asked Der Platoniker, "with your son, I mean?"

"He and Mousy got up—in a huff, I might add—and said they would be writing to the administration. What are they hoping to do? Have us all put in straitjackets? As they were leaving, I suggested that maybe they needed to get his *schmeckle* out more often and they wouldn't be so uptight!"

"Oh, Schwanzie, you are so *drôle!*" Keska Saye reached over and played with a twist of Schwanzie's hair. Der Platoniker took note.

"Who's Rocky arguing with?" asked Twilight.

"Rocky" was the Woods-name for Martin Smith. His family had known him as a soft-spoken, easy-going social worker, one never given to swearing or fighting. But now he was Rocky. The oldest among the residents thought the name came from Rocky Marciano, a world heavyweight champion during the early 1950s. The younger residents believed his Woods-name came from the series of Sylvester Stallone films from the late 1970s and early 1980s. Of course, the origin of the name didn't actually matter at Carolina Woods; the former mild-mannered Martin Smith was now the pugnacious Rocky. Despite being in his early seventies, he was in very good physical condition. His five-foot-nine-inch frame was largely muscle, as compared to most of the residents. This was perhaps due to his running five miles every day and working out in the community's exercise room, where he had his own punching bag.

During his regular jogs, Rocky could be heard taunting his invisible opponents: "C'mon! Ya scared of me? Let's see what you're made of!" Often Rocky's unseen opponents bore the names of public figures—the president, some senators and even Hollywood stars. Donald Trump was one of his favorite targets: "C'mon, you big tub of lard. Think you're a man? You ain't got nothing! *Nothing*—ya hear me?!" This was harmless enough, but problems occurred whenever Rocky saw himself in a mirror—such as those which lined one wall of the exercise room. Like a budgerigar which is attracted to its image, Rocky would, upon catching the first glimpse of himself, start an argument. "Come on, you sorry sombitch! You want it, do ya? Well, I'm waiting, so bring it on!" Of course, the Rocky in the mirror never answered back, so it would become a long-lasting stalemate until a staff member could distract him. This was often best accomplished by placing a picture of one of Rocky's nemeses on the punching bag, and then calling attention to it.

"Hey, Rocky! You gonna let Senator Burr say that to you?" Rocky would then abandon his image for the face on the bag, which would soon become tattered pulp. The community's physical therapist and physical activity instructor was amazed at how long, and with such a steady rhythm, Rocky could punch the bag. He averred to his colleagues that he would never want to step into the ring with Rocky—septuagenarian or not!

On this particular evening, as darkness was falling, Rocky had seen his image in a window of the dining hall. Twilight had seen him begin his verbal jousting with the mute image. Smooth as glass, Richard Wilson—one of the staff members—slipped between Rocky and his image. "Rocky, my man! That guy ain't no match for you, bro!

But if you plan to tangle with somebody, you gotta eat. Right?" Rocky smiled and patted the care assistant on the shoulder.

"Sure, man, you're right. I gotta stay fit—'cause you never know."

"That's right, bro, you never know! Let's get your dinner and find you a seat."

Twilight, who had watched with curiosity the proceedings with Rocky, mused aloud, "Maybe we should have boxing lessons during our morning exercise class?"

"Yeah, right," replied Schwanzie. "Who can afford the new dentures and hearing aids? And over half of us have prostheses of some description or other. Boxing lessons! Rocky would slaughter the lot of us!" Twilight just smiled, pleased with her idea.

Der Platoniker wanted to change the subject. "Keska?"

"Yes, dahling?"

"Have you found your dream life more...well, especially colorful after the Saturday Surprise?"

"Oh Plato, I have found my dream-life positively *formidable* since coming to live here. Haven't you?"

"Yes, I suppose I have. I...er, find myself having conversations with Martin Heidegger and Ludwig Wittgenstein, among others."

"And who are they, dahling?"

"Well, one was a fucking Nazi," interjected Schwanzie.

"Which one was that?" enquired Keska.

"Heidegger," grimaced Schwanzie. "As for the other," he held out his right hand and wiggled it back and forth, "Whereof one cannot speak, thereof one must be silent."

"How profound, Schwanzie!" admired Keska.

"That was Wittgenstein," said Der Platoniker.

"No, dear Plato, I heard it quite distinctly from Schwanzie. He's sitting right here!"

Der Platoniker lifted his hand and started to protest, but decided he wouldn't bother.

"So Platoniker," Schwanzie said. "What do you and Heidegger get up to? Does he share with you his thoughts on 'How I got ahead by joining the Nazi party?'"

"No actually, that would be more in line with Mach Schnell's interests. I...um, chat with Heidegger about 'is-ness.'"

"Is-ness?" asked Schwanzie in disbelief. "*Is-ness*? Is-ness schmizness! I'd wake up with a goddamned headache if I had dreams like that! You know we have some retired psychiatrists here? Go speak with Sigmund over there. I'm sure he'd help cure you of dreams about Nazi philosophers."

Somewhat embarrassed, Der Platoniker replied, "Well, it was Keska Saye who asked me about my dreams. And Heidegger and I never speak about politics. *Es ist ganz verboten*...um, that is, it is a forbidden topic in our little group."

"And what about the other gentleman, Lichtenstein?" Keska asked.

"Wittgenstein!" snapped Schwanzie. At that moment all their attention was focused upon a splashing noise. Twilight had fallen sound asleep face-first into her dinner plate. Schwanzie shook her gently. "Twilight, sweetie, wake up!"

Twilight awoke with a surprised expression on her face. "What was the choice of vegetables again?" she smiled.

"They're on your face. Come on, Twilight, let's go back to the apartment. It's time for bed." Schwanzie helped the bemused Twilight to her feet and wiped her face with a napkin.

"And I think I was having the most pleasant dream," said Twilight, as she was ushered away by her husband. "I was a rutabaga about to go into a nice pot of boiling stew..."

Two

The Kids Call In: Rocky

"So Dad, how are things?"

"Rocky...please call me Rocky."

"Now Father, you know Jason and I can't call you Rocky," Maryanne said in a saccharine voice. "You're his father and my lovely father-in-law." Turning to her husband, Maryanne asked, "What is it with this place? Everyone we've met has some crazy nickname."

Jason gave a pained expression, as he silently mouthed, "Dementia?" He tried once more with his father. "Look Dad, I know—"

"Rocky, goddamnit! Are ya hard of hearing?"

"Really Martin, there's no need to swear!" interrupted Maryanne, "You never swore until you came here!" She primly tried to smooth out non-existent wrinkles in her dress.

Rocky pointed at Maryanne as he said to his son, "She wants a good smack in da mouth."

Jason dropped his head into his hands. "Okay, okay. Rocky, how is your life here at Carolina Woods? You're looking the best I have seen since before Mom died. What's the secret?"

Rocky slapped his pectoral muscles and said, "Working out and running five miles every day. Wouldn't hurt you none." Rocky poked at his son's middle-aged flab.

"I get enough exercise, Dad—er, I mean Rocky." Jason smiled weakly. "I cut the grass every week in the warm months, rake leaves in the autumn, help with the washing and ironing—"

Jason was interrupted by his father. Jerking his thumb at Maryanne, he asked, "She give you any for doing all of that?"

"Give me any *what*?"

"*Any what*? Do I gotta spell it out for you? Pussy, sex, poontang. I mean, how often do you unwrap that package? She ain't bad lookin', ya know."

"Da-ad," whined Jason, "Maryanne can hear you. She's sitting right here."

"Goddamnit, I ain't blind, ya know! You two are wound up tighter than a three-dollar watch! A little sex wouldn't do yous no harm and would probably do ya a lot of good!"

Maryanne's peaches and cream complexion had, by this time, morphed into a shade of a garden-variety beetroot. The slightest hint of perspiration had begun to appear on her brow and she dabbed at it nervously with her handkerchief.

Reaching out and taking Maryanne's arm, Rocky, *sotto voce*, offered her his counsel. "Look, sweetheart, if Junior here isn't taking care of your womanly needs, we got a fellow here named Schwanzie. He might be old, but he has a pecker about yay long." Rocky measured out his hands for emphasis. "And rumor has it that he has satisfied a lot of the ladies here...Whas wrong?!"

Maryanne's head had drooped between her knees. "Honey, what is it?" asked a concerned Jason.

A muffled voice replied, "I think I'm going to faint."

Rocky sat back in his chair, shaking his head. "Jeez, women today!" Then, punching Jason on the shoulder, he added, "Son, when your mother and I were your age, we went at it like rabbits! If my memory serves me, you were conceived on the kitchen table—you remember, the one you used to do your homework on?"

"Jesus Christ, Dad!" Helping Maryanne to her feet, Jason spoke over his shoulder. "We're leaving now, Dad—"

"Rocky, damn it! How many times I gotta tell ya?"

Jason began crying. He and Maryanne made a perfect A-frame as they supported one another. Sobbing, Jason blubbered out, "I-I just d-don't know what's happened t-to you here. Where is t-the father y-you used to be?"

"Right here, ya candy-ass! Maybe the man I used to be was a wimpy social worker. But the question ain't what's happened to me, it oughta be what's happened to *you*?! She's the one with da pussy and here you are whining like a baby girl!"

Summoning her courage, Maryanne erupted. "Rocky! I mean *Dad*, really! Must you be so...so awful? We're only here because we care for you!" Jason and Maryanne shuffled to the door, each with handkerchiefs over their faces.

Jason fumbled with the doorknob. With his back turned, he managed his voice enough to say, "I don't know when we'll be back..."

As the couple proceeded out the door, a puzzled Rocky called after them, "Hey, what happened to lunch?"

Three

Dangerous Denizens of the Woods

Der Platoniker was taking his evening walk when he spotted Great White moving stealthily from one tree to another. Great White was a retired businessman who had led several insurance brokerages to their financial ruin due to his preference for big game hunting, which had consumed most of the profits. His long-suffering wife, Janet, whose Woods name was Choo-choo, because she smoked like a steam train (her single occupation), had managed to secure a place at Carolina Woods only by assiduously protecting an inheritance from her parents over the last thirty years. She had nearly given GW a stroke when she informed him that their apartment at The Woods would not be large enough to accommodate his 'trophies,' which consisted of various animal parts which had undergone their transformation into grotesque caricatures of themselves through the agency of a taxidermist. Great White was short for Great White Hunter, as you might have guessed, which most of his fellow residents found too cumbersome to pronounce. There were some who simply accorded him the initials GW.

On this autumn evening, the humid air carried the scent of pine sap along the lugubrious breeze. Just as Der Platoniker was about to greet Great White, GW spotted him and frantically waved one hand to signal 'slow down' while with the other he placed his index finger over his lips, making a shss-ing sound. Der Platoniker stopped in his tracks, looking here and there to discern the apparent danger or whatever it might be that caused Great White such anxiety. Seeing that Der Platoniker had stopped completely in the open, Great White urgently pointed toward a tree, signaling that Der Platoniker should hide. Great White pointed to his ears and then nodded toward the darkening woods. Der Platoniker shrugged and whispered, "What gives?"

GW looked at his fellow resident as though he were mad, nodding again toward the thicker growth of trees and pointing at both ears. Der Platoniker pointed to his ears and shook his head. Great White peeked around the tree trunk and then beckoned Der Platoniker to join him. Not knowing exactly why, Der Platoniker found himself tiptoeing to the adjacent tree. When he was an arm's length from GW, the latter reached out, grabbed him by his shirt and pulled him close. "Can't you *hear* them?"

"Hear what?" queried Der Platoniker.

By now GW was in near exasperation. "*The drums!* Can't you hear them? They are coming from just over there." Not wanting to expose his position, GW peeped around the tree, looked back at Der Platoniker and pointed with his finger. Der Platoniker slowly put his head to the side of their shared tree, peering into the shadows, all the while cupping his hand around his left ear, trying to make out any drumlike sounds. After a few moments, he turned back toward an expectant Great White, who said, "See what I mean?!"

"Sorry GW, but I can't hear anything like drums. Are you sure you weren't hearing Interstate Forty through the woods? The sound really carries at night. But anyway, why are you hiding from the sound of drums?"

"I'm not hiding from the sound of drums, you idiot! I am not wanting to make myself an easy target!"

"GW, are you all right? I mean, who would want to target you?"

"The Pygmies! Do you mean to tell me you've never seen or heard them?"

Der Platoniker shook his head, looking askance at Great White. "GW, are you drunk—or stoned?" It was an open secret that a fair number of residents regularly smoked dope, Der Platoniker included—but not this evening.

"Very funny," snapped GW. "But look at this." With a flourish, he produced from his pocket a handkerchief, which appeared to be wrapped around some object. He gingerly unwound it and exclaimed, "*Voilá!*"

"A broken chopstick?" asked Der Platoniker.

"Don't be ridiculous!" snapped Great White. "It's a blow dart. Any *idiot* can see that!"

That's for sure, thought Der Platoniker. "Forgive me for asking, but if it's a blow dart, where are its feathers?"

"You've watched too many Tarzan movies," grumbled GW. "Remember, I've spent time in Africa. Have you?"

"Well as a matter of fact—" began Der Platoniker, but GW cut him off.

"Never mind." GW turned his face toward the now sunless woods. "He said he would get me one day..." Great White's voice trailed away.

Der Platoniker was torn between wanting to finish his walk and wanting to hear more of the 'stoned rap' coming from Great White. "Okay, I'll bite," said Der Platoniker. "Who said he'd get you one day?"

"This little chieftain guy of the whatddaya call 'em?...Oh yeah, the Bambuti—they're a Pygmy tribe in the Congo. He got all hot and bothered because I shot some elephant they seemed to revere. I dunno, maybe he thought it was his grandfather or something. Anyway, he was jabbering away at me as my team cut off the head—and man, you shoulda seen those tusks!—so I pointed my rifle at the chieftain and asked my interpreter to tell him that if he didn't shut his trap, I'd put *his* head on my trophy wall. He then made some sign, babbled something in his language and left. That evening my curiosity got the better of me, so I asked the interpreter what the little guy had said. He told me the chieftain had put some sort of curse on me...that even if I crossed the ocean, the curse would track me down, so I would become the hunted game."

With the nightfall, there came the unwelcome hum of mosquitoes who honed in on the two stationary blood banks. "Damn it," cursed Der Platoniker as he slapped his arm after being bitten. He was cross that his evening walk was at an end as the mosquitoes closed in on him and Great White. Waving them away from his ears and face, Der Platoniker bade Great White Hunter adieu and turned to walk away. As an afterthought, he called over his shoulder, "You know, I had to take some Percodan once for a slipped disc. I hallucinated like I never did on acid. You might want to check your meds, GW."

As Der Platoniker returned to his cottage, he did notice some-thing—or rather *someone*—in the woods. It seemed to be a caped fig-ure, dashing from tree to tree.

Four

The Divinity Student

Jimmy T. Watkins was positively brimming with good will for his fellow man...well, for his fellow woman, too, but his Southern Baptist ethos preferred the masculine 'man' as encompassing women as well. But you know what I'm talking about, don't you? Jimmy, or Jimmy T, as he was variously known, was a divinity student at a nearby Southern Baptist seminary. Jimmy was his given name, not James, as one might think, because his parents had decided they were going to call him Jimmy regardless, so why bother with the more formal—or even biblical—James? Jimmy T was also a good ol' boy. Perhaps this is a fact that does not need stating, for how many writers, scientists, architects or statesmen of note go by their first name and middle initial? If you are thinking of George W. Bush, or "Dubya," then I rest my case.

Jimmy T was in his final year of seminary and had been assigned to Carolina Woods as his field education for the year. He arrived with all of the usual eagerness of divinity students approaching their ordination. In less than a year, he would have conferred upon him the ecclesiastical authority over the Christian rites of passage, whereby the faithful are hatched, matched and dispatched. Prior to being loosed upon the 'congregation' at The Woods, Jimmy had to pass muster with both the CEO, Beatrice Charon, and Gretchen Beauxreves, clinical psychologist and director of resident services. To save time, the two women decided to interview Jimmy together. Over the last few years, they had decided to alternate between Methodist and Baptist divinity students. They joked that it took the Methodists' focus upon grace to put right the ruffled feathers of the residents after eight months of rigid moral certainties and muted threats of damnation from the Baptist students.

Beatrice and Gretchen met over coffee to go over Jimmy's CV prior to his arrival. The former was a self-proclaimed agnostic, while the latter was a liberal Episcopalian. As a result, they tended to agree on their approach. It was patently clear to both women that the residents of The Woods were more than capable both of genuinely welcoming divinity students and of handling some of the more ardent types, usually coming from the Baptist seminary. The two colleagues had their motto for the student chaplains: "Pastoral care, not proselytizing." This was their one hard and fast rule, and they tolerated no breaches. Those students who came to collect scalps for Christ were soon looking for another field placement. For his previous field education, Jimmy had served as chaplain to a fire department, where he had been given a largely positive evaluation and a fire-engine-red racing-style jacket, with his name and position embroidered in gold thread. Jimmy had proudly worn the coat since leaving the field placement as it, for him, conferred both honor and status.

When Beatrice's administrative assistant called her to announce Mr. Watkins' arrival, they both stood and prepared to greet the young man. What they could not be prepared for was the fact that Jimmy T was the youthful living image of Jim Bakker, disgraced TV evangelist and convicted fraudster. In addition, he was wearing his bright red fire-service jacket. Neither woman could control the look of shock on her face and—although they were eloquent speakers—both stammered and looked to her colleague to speak first. Happily, Jimmy T had taken no notice of their dismay and thrust his hand forward to Gretchen, as she was the closer. "Mornin' ma'am, I'm so pleased to meet you!"

While Gretchen introduced herself and her role at The Woods, Beatrice was recovering from shock. But then, under Jimmy T's name, she noticed **Chaplin** emblazoned in gold thread on the left breast of the coat. We don't always know why we find things funny; it's probably more the case that they find us. When asked to explain jazz, Louis Armstrong purportedly answered, "If ya gotta ask, don't mess with it." In any case, Beatrice knew she was about to burst out laughing at the malapropism. She knew it was inappropriate; she knew it was unprofessional; she knew it might hurt Jimmy's feelings, as he proudly wore the jacket seemingly unawares. Suddenly, in a stroke of genius, Beatrice feigned a small cough, turned toward her desk and grabbed her coffee mug just as the image of Charlie Chaplin's little tramp sprang fully into mind. As she gulped the coffee, the laugh exploded—as did the coffee, everywhere. Covering her mouth and waving her hand at Gretchen—which was supposed to mean 'carry on,' Beatrice dashed to the ladies' room in Olympic time. She turned on both taps and flushed both toilets to cover her laughter. Every time she thought she had herself under control, the Charlie Chaplin in her mind's eye would twitch his mustache or twirl his walking stick. Once that image was subdued, her pedantic side would rear its head and whisper, "What kind of twit would proudly wear a jacket with 'Chaplin' embroidered on it?" She wasn't enamored with that aspect of herself, and had dealt with it in therapy, but in the end, it did suit her to work in an environment with highly educated people. Leaning over one of the hand basins, Beatrice did her best to repair her make-up—*sans* handbag—with a dampened paper towel.

The restroom door opened and Gretchen peeped in. "Are you okay?"

"Getting there," responded Beatrice.

"Were you choking or *what*?"

"*What.* Just don't ask me about it right now. I'll explain later. How's the Bakker lookalike doing?"

"You think so, too?!" asked Gretchen. "It's incredible. You think he's Bakker's love child?"

"The way that so-called Christian *evangelist* put it around, who knows? He was more of a Christian *vaginist!*" Both women laughed.

Just then another head joined Gretchen's. It was the admin assistant, Karen. "Uh, ladies? Mr. Watkins has asked me if he should come back another time...um...what should I tell him?" Then looking at her boss, she added, "And what the hell happened to you? I've never seen you move so fast!"

"Later. Must tell you later," mumbled Beatrice as she finished repairing her makeup and hair. Then she added, "Just be glad I didn't pee myself as well! Tell Mr. Watkins I choked on my coffee."

Karen shook her head in a puzzled fashion and strode back to the office. As Gretchen and Beatrice were returning to the interview, they looked at one another and grinned. "Not another word!" whispered Beatrice as she sought to regain her professional self.

Jimmy T stood as the women entered and looked somewhat goggle-eyed as he asked, "Mrs. Charon, um...?"

"Ms." smiled Beatrice confidently.

"Oh yes, um, Ms. Charon, are you okay?"

"Couldn't be better. Just a little mishap. I trust you're happy to continue?" Jimmy nodded. "Okay then, why don't you tell us a bit about why you'd like the student chaplaincy post at Carolina Woods for this academic year and what you hope to gain from it? Have you a particular interest in working with older adults?"

"Well, I don't exactly plan to work with older adults as a focus for my ministry, but I have always enjoyed being around older people, like my grandparents. I like hearing about their lives. But I also reckon there are some folks who get to this stage of life and might have worries about...well, death...and um...what the future holds for them. I'd like to think I could bring some comfort to them. And when I get my own church, well, I'll being working with folks of all ages, so I think this will help me." Jimmy paused to get a sense of how he was doing.

Beatrice found that by staring at the tip of Jimmy's nose, it kept her from seeing him as his partial namesake, Jimmy Bakker. She also hoped it might actually appear she was looking him in the eye. *So far, so good.*

"Jimmy, please tell me what you mean by what the future holds for people with regard to death."

Jimmy swallowed. This was what he had been prepared for at the seminary: Liberals! Liberals who, if they had any notion of 'heaven,' it was as an amorphous, disease and death-free afterlife, wherein all sins (or misdeeds!) were forgotten and people pretty much carried on as they had in the flesh. *How to be truthful, but without using the other 'H-word': Hell?* Jimmy felt himself starting to perspire. He fiddled with his collar and quickly wiped his hand across his upper lip to capture any beads of sweat. "We-ell," he drawled, sucking in lungs-full of air, "Y'all obviously know I am a Christian and we believe that... well, as a person lives—or lived—affects how they...um, experience the afterlife. And this can bother some folks. Or if they ain—" Jimmy caught himself and pretended to cough, "if they *aren't* exactly worried, they maybe still have some questions about faith and what death holds...um...for them." Jimmy smiled weakly and ended his faltering discourse, having decided he had better not say too much.

Feeling a little wicked, Beatrice teased Jimmy, "So, you have experienced the afterlife?" She looked at him, poker-faced.

Jimmy's mouth dropped open gormlessly. "Um...well no...that is, not exactly...um, what I mean is that I *believe in* an afterlife. I...uh..." His voice trailed away.

Beatrice chuckled out loud. "I apologize, Jimmy. I was just messing with you. But it is something you'll have to get used to here at The Woods. Not all are professing Christians...there are some Jews and a fair number of atheists and agnostics. Some will not want your services and others will enjoy intellectual jousting with you. Do you think you're up for that?"

"Yes ma'am, I believe I am." Jimmy nodded earnestly.

Beatrice continued, "We have one hard and fast rule here: no proselytizing. You are here for pastoral care and the provision of

Christian worship. Anyone you see has to be on a voluntary basis. Is that understood?"

Now nodding in overdrive, Jimmy replied, "Yessum, I understand completely."

"On a day-to-day basis and for your supervision, you'll report to Ms. Beauxreves. But I would like to hear from you, say, four times during your fieldwork here, starting six weeks after you start. Ms. Beauxreves will show you the auditorium, which doubles as a chapel on Sundays and holy days, and we have a spare office here in the admin building that you can use as an office whenever you're here." Jimmy was still nodding. Beatrice wondered whether he had a spring in his neck like those little puppies that people put in the rear windows of their cars. She quickly put the thought out of her mind, knowing that the combination of Jim Bakker's face mixed with a spring-loaded puppy figure would send her into hysterics again. Drinking some water to hide her burgeoning smile, she added, "Jimmy, there is one more thing. The jacket." Jimmy stared at the garment that was his pride and joy. "It's not going to work here."

While Beatrice debated whether or not to point out the misspelling of 'chaplain,' Gretchen noticed it for the first time. Now she knew what had set off Beatrice's fit of laughter. Stifling her own, she uttered a sound somewhat like that of a guinea pig being squeezed too tightly by a child. Reflexively, both Jimmy and Beatrice turned toward Gretchen, who waved a hand at them while squeaking, "Allergies!"

Beatrice took the opportunity to stand abruptly and walk to a cabinet where spare keys were kept. Through tightened jaws and lips, she managed to expel a few words, "Just finding your keys, Mr. Watkins." Though they were all clearly labeled, she rummaged around in the drawer, giving herself time to wipe the huge grin from her face. She knew what Gretchen was going through, but decided to leave said colleague to her own devices. Feeling safe, Beatrice turned back to Jimmy, hoping her smile would be taken as one of collegiality, while Gretchen made grunts and squeaky noises into her handkerchief. Handing the keys to Jimmy, Beatrice explained, "The larger one is for the main door to this building, the smaller is for your office, which Ms. Beauxreves will show you shortly...when she recovers from her allergy attack. And I believe that will be all from me for now." She remained standing so Jimmy would get the message.

Jimmy stood, nodded yet again, saying, "Thank you, Mrs-um... *Ms.* Charon. I won't let you down."

"Glad to hear it." Beatrice nodded 'over to you' to Gretchen, who gently wiped her eyes and blew her nose, before standing and motioning Jimmy toward the door. Following him out, Gretchen looked over her shoulder and mouthed, "Chaplin," shaking her head and quickly closing the door behind her. She set off at a brisk pace, mainly to keep Jimmy somewhat behind her as she struggled to regain control of her facial muscles. Within seconds, they were at the office Jimmy would use.

"You have the keys," she stated as they stood before the locked door.

"Oh!" Jimmy looked at his right hand which held the keys and then immediately used the wrong one.

"That's for the main door," offered Gretchen. Jimmy nervously placed the second key into the lock and opened the door. There was a bare desk with a swivel chair, an armchair, small settee and a few framed photos on the walls of The Woods in different seasons.

"This'll do fine," said Jimmy. "Is it all right if I bring in a few things of mine?"

"Certainly. It will be yours from now until the end of April. Shall I show you where the auditorium is?"

"Yes, ma'am!"

"Jimmy? You don't have to keep calling me 'ma'am.' I'm not your mama."

"How should I call you?"

"Anything but *collect*," quipped Gretchen.

Being too young to comprehend the joke, Jimmy blurted, "Come again?"

"Gretchen will suffice."

"Um, okay, thanks."

As they approached the door to the auditorium, Schwanzie was entering the front door. Torn between her natural desire to greet a resident and get Jimmy out of a potential line of fire, she made the mistake of looking toward Schwanzie too long. "Gretch, good morning! *Nu*? Who's the newbie? Don't tell me The Woods is accepting juvenile residents!"

Before she could introduce the student chaplain, Jimmy had stepped forward with hand out held, "Hi, I'm Jimmy Watkins. I'll be serving as chaplain for the next eight months."

And then it happened: while taking Jimmy's hand, Schwanzie noticed the **Chaplin** on his jacket. He twitched his mustache back and forth and quipped, "Modern times, eh? Will you deliver your sermons in subtitles? Anyway, gotta dash. See you in the pictures!"

"Whu—" was all Jimmy's mouth and brain could manage. Wide-eyed and pie-faced, he watched Schwanzie stroll down the hallway, in Chaplin's penguin-style walk. He turned to Gretchen, quizzically searching her face.

Gretchen simply shrugged and said, "Jewish humor...you'll get used to it." Then added, *sotto voce*, "I hope."

Five

The Recital

On at least a monthly basis, Gretchen Beauxreves arranged for one of the residents to give a talk on a special interest, read poetry, or to sing or perform on a musical instrument, if so talented. It usually followed the Saturday dinner, as that was the one meal regularly eaten communally by the residents of The Woods, and thus they would all be in the main building. On this particular evening, the performance would be by Mach Schnell. As Mach was not known to be the friendliest of residents, the audience was largely comprised of the curious. The program leaflet was scanty at best, simply stating that there would be an evening of German Lieder. The accompanist was a retired professor of music, simply known as "Keys," as she volunteered to play at social gatherings, worship services and the like. Sight-reading music presented no problems for her. Keys was diminutive, with a thick shock of greying curly, red hair and a still shapely body for her seventy-three years. Schwanzie had offered to turn the pages for her, but seemed more attentive to her cleavage as he stood by the piano.

Things began as one might have expected. Mach had decided to perform in black tie, a little over-the-top for the relaxed atmosphere at The Woods, but such was his prerogative. He carried a briefcase from which he produced the sheet music for each song. Mach commenced with Schubert's "Die Forelle" and his aging tenor voice did credibly well. There followed "Der Lindenbaum," "Der Wanderer," "Nacht und Träume." But then things took a somewhat darker tone with "Der Er-lkönig," which, if you are not familiar with it, is based on a ballad by Goethe and relates the story of a father on horseback with his seriously ill son. The son sees the approach of the "Erl King"—a mysterious elf-like creature who beckons the boy to accompany him, but to his death. The father believes the son to be delirious, but when he arrives at his destination, the child is dead. For this literate audience, who themselves were also closer to death—not to mention the impassioned theatrics of Mach—the mood took a certain downward dip.

Mach pulled a handkerchief from his sleeve and mopped his face before striding to his briefcase and pulling out the next song. As Keys placed the sheets on the music holder, Schwanzie's brow furrowed and he mumbled something to Keys. Keys simply shrugged and began playing. In an already pensive mood, Mach began singing, *"Ich hatt' einen Kameraden,"* which had served as the German army's funeral song in various wars, but most notoriously as the background music to the reading of casualty lists by Joseph Goebbel's ministry of propaganda in the Second World War. By the time Mach sang the final words, he was in tears, while Schwanzie's contorted face looked as though he had just drunk cod-liver oil and lemon juice.

But then, with chest thrust forward, Mach strode to the edge of the stage and, singing *a cappella*, belted out *"Die Fahne hoch! Die Reihen fest geschlossen! SA marschiert..."* at which Schwanzie exploded. There were also shocked groans of recognition from much of the audience.

"That's the fucking Nazi party's song, you stupid prick! Are you a fucking Nazi!?"

At this moment, Twilight, who was gently dozing in the front row, piped up. "We hate fucking Nazis, dear. Why would we fuck Nazis? We're Jews."

Meanwhile, a struggle had broken out on stage between Mach and Schwanzie, with various insults being growled at each other... "Jewish pig!" "Stupid Nazi fuck!" as they struggled to remove the other from the stage. By then, Gretchen Beauxreves was climbing the stairs on stage right, not noticing that Rocky had already mounted the stage from the left. Gretchen might have been sprightly, but Rocky was faster. Just as Mach, who towered over Schwanzie, drew back his right fist, Rocky's left hand grabbed and pinned it back while his right landed squarely on Mach's nose. The crack of breaking cartilage could be heard throughout most of the auditorium, swiftly followed by the visible trail of blood.

"Take that, you Nazi scum! Your pals killed my uncle Murray in the Ardennes, you sombitch!" Mach slipped to the floor, resting on his backside, holding his nose with his right hand, while supporting himself by his left arm. Dazed, he removed his hand and stared in disbelief at the copious amount of blood, which had by then also soaked his crisp, white shirt. Meanwhile, Rocky was dancing in place, making short jabs as he looked down at Mach, "Ready for annudda round, ya fuckin' Nazi?"

By then, several of the kitchen staff had responded to the hubbub and joined Gretchen in helping to calm the situation. Richard, who always had a good way with Rocky, eased alongside him, saying, "Rocky, the champ! Man, that's a TKO! He's down for the count. Come over here and tell me all about it."

The general disapprobation of the remainder of the audience, along with hearing the mention of "Nazi songs" from several of them, told Gretchen that Mach had overstepped the mark—big time. Taking his arm, she helped the still-stunned Mach to his feet and said, "Let's go to the infirmary."

"*Lass mich in Ruhe!*" Mach jerked his arm away.

Having enough college German to understand the rebuff, Gretchen tightened her grip and growled, "That wasn't an invitation, asshole!

And cool it with the German!" She signaled to Marvin, the building custodian, to join her in case Mach proved to be unruly. Marvin Hendricks was a disabled vet from the Gulf War. He stood about six-foot-three and weighed two-hundred and thirty-five pounds. Marvin had a prosthetic leg—but one would hardly notice it from the way he carried himself. His biceps were the size of Mach's thigh muscles. Marvin was well-trained in restraint techniques, particularly for patients who became violent due to dementia or medications. His hands were the equivalent of a human straitjacket. Secretly Gretchen delighted in the fact that Mach was being escorted by an African-American. *Suck it up, white boy!*

At the door, Gretchen stopped and looked for Schwanzie and Keys. They had descended the stage, so she left Mach with Marvin and went to ask them to accompany her to the infirmary, where they could discuss the offending events while Mach was checked over by a nurse. Schwanzie agreed to come as soon as he had Twilight back in their apartment. Complacent Keys simply smiled and followed along.

Outside the examination room, a near-breathless Schwanzie joined Gretchen and Keys. "So, what exactly happened?" queried Gretchen.

Keys, who remembered the language of music, but was losing the art of daily discourse, smiled and shrugged. "I played what that man gave me. Is that all right?" She looked adoringly at Schwanzie, who smiled in return.

Gretchen patted Keys' hand and said, "You did just as you were asked. Thank you." Then, turning to Schwanzie, "What gives?"

"That schmuck Schnell didn't give Keys the music in advance. He just sprang it on her—and me. He sang a couple of Nazi songs—in particular the Horst Wessel Lied. That was the goddamned anthem of the Nazi party! What kind of anti-Semite jerk does that kind of thing today?—in America?"

"Probably more than we know or would like to know," moaned Gretchen. "Surely you've seen the news."

"*Nu*, and what's with this German accent he uses? He's as American-born as you and I are!"

"Look, Schwanzie, surely you know that people here tend to let out their...what shall I say, their alter-ego or perhaps their true inner person? But don't get too exercised over this. I'll talk with Beatrice later and we'll put Mach on warning. One more stunt like tonight's and he's out of here. Trust me. Mach's on a short leash. Why don't you and Keys go on home?"

Schwanzie stood and proffered his arm to Keys, who positively beamed as she took it. "May I escort you home?"

Gretchen thought in that moment Schwanzie sounded more like Rhett Butler than a New Yorker from the Bronx. She cocked her head and smiled inwardly.

As for Keys, she merely giggled and said, "Delighted."

Six

The Juice

The Juice was the Woods-name for Bruce Bland, a wannabe New Yorker who actually hailed from Hackensack, New Jersey. He was originally called Bruce-the-Juice, but as things happened at The Woods, it quickly morphed into The Juice. He was a lush who had made a niche for himself in North Carolina's blossoming wine industry, writing a column which appeared in a few local newspapers. The small income largely kept him in drink when the freebies from the local winegrowers ran dry—which was often. In retirement, it was largely his adult children who paid for his apartment at The Woods, with their efforts augmented by The Juice's Social Security payments and a small work pension.

Schwanzie averred that The Juice was such a *goyische kop* that his own kids couldn't stand to be around him, so they 'sentenced him' to a retirement community—far from them! "In fact," stated Schwanzie, "It's we who have been sentenced to The Juice!"

"Bland by name, bland by nature," agreed Der Platoniker.

The Juice fancied himself a delightfully knowledgeable raconteur; whereas in fact his need to let people know *what he thought he knew* made him an excruciating bore. (You're thinking of someone just like that right now, aren't you?) The Juice was built like an inchworm climbing a wall. Which is to say, he had a tall, skinny frame which bulged in the middle due both to his wine consumption and his lack of exercise. His six-foot-five height only added to peoples' sense of being 'talked down to,' but it did have the advantage of making his approach easily spotted by those who wished to avoid his company. Residents were known to barge into apartments of people they barely knew in order to avoid being stopped in their tracks while The Juice poured his words over them like an oil slick.

About every six months, The Juice would organize a wine-tasting at The Woods, sponsored by a number of wineries in North Carolina's Piedmont. He gave the same old spiel each time, so those who attended were either new to the community or simply there for the free wine-bibbing—none more so than The Juice himself. The admin staff at The Woods would often humor him by letting him print a dozen or so flyers announcing his wine tastings. It wasn't enough for The Juice that they would appear on both the monthly and weekly activities lists, which were posted in every lobby. He liked to shove them into the hands of unsuspecting passersby. Great White was usually a sitting target, as he would often be found behind a tree, just off a footpath dodging the Pygmy blow darts. The Juice nailed him on a glorious autumn morning, completely ignoring GW's efforts to warn him of imminent danger. "Whatever," was all he got from The Juice, who pushed a leaflet into the unwilling hand of Great White.

The Juice took no heed of the danger proclaimed by GW in the same way he heard nothing of interest from *any* of the other residents. Unlike many older people who have mellowed with the years, The Juice had distilled into a potent vintage of rancid vinegar, with which he liberally doused his fellow human beings. Neither fear of death nor even the faintest hint of mortality played any part in The Juice's consciousness—particularly in a retirement community—because, as the center of his universe, he was the prime observer without whose purview nothing would or could exist. Don't tell me you've never met anyone like that! If anyone were unlucky enough to be cornered by The Juice, any attempted getaway was impeded by the fact that The Juice would hold their arm, just above the elbow. Like so many of the great jazz artists who played wind instruments, The Juice had seemingly developed the talent for circular breathing, because he could speak without ostensibly taking a breath. This prevented any of his victims from getting a word in edgewise—from "I need the toilet!" to "I'm deaf, you great oaf!"

Schwanzie and Der Platoniker had begun a private competition writing limericks about The Juice. They determined that humor was their best weapon for dealing with a bore. Having successfully dodged The Juice's leafleting, Der Platoniker spouted forth:

There was once a man of ill-humor

Whose life was one drunken stupor.

His mind was fermented,

His harangues were demented,

He was truly one great party-pooper.

"That's good! That's very good! I like it. What say we print some of these up and hand them out as a counterbalance to The Juice? *Nu?*"

"I'm tempted, but I prefer something more subversive." Der Platoniker gazed into the woods deep in thought.

"So spill it!"

"Before The Juice's wine-tasting performances, he always opens the bottles to let them breathe, right?"

"Yeah, so?"

"What if we pulled the old switcheroo on him? We create some sort of distraction to get him out of the dining hall while he's setting up, then pour out most of the good wine into decanters while adding cheap plonk into what's left."

"That's pure genius! But we're gonna need more help to spirit away the good stuff, aren't we?"

"You're probably right, but can you imagine anyone in The Woods who wouldn't gladly help us? Your car or mine?"

"*Nu*, mine's closer. Let's hit that convenience store just along the road from here. It's bound to have some really bad stuff—MD20/20—it's kosher, you know—and Thunderbird! Ha!"

Five minutes later, the two curmudgeons were in the local filling station's convenience store. The young man at the checkout picked his nose while he watched the two elderly gentlemen discussing the chilled wines and laughing hysterically. He was beginning to take them for a couple of old winos, particularly when they appeared at the cash register with numerous bottles of cheap wine. The co-conspirators were still giggling as they each searched for their wallets. "Allow me, please," offered Schwanzie, as he produced the cash with a flourish.

The nose-picker chimed in. "You guys having a party or somethin'?"

"Something," replied Schwanzie.

"It's sort of a surprise," added Der Platoniker. He chuckled.

After he had rung up each bottle, the young man asked, "Um... y'all want these in paper bags?"

"Strictly speaking, good sir, the etiquette for brown paper bags states that they are to be used *specifically* when drinking wine in doorways and on park benches. But, yes, we'll make this an exception and have the bags," spoke Schwanzie.

The store attendant's mouth hung open for a moment while his brain tried to assimilate brown bag etiquette. As his two customers were older, neatly dressed and he assumed wiser about such subjects, he asked, "Um, is that like...you know, for real?"

"Absolutely!" added Der Platoniker. "Research has clearly proven that ninety-seven point eight per cent of small brown paper bags are correctly used by winos, degenerates and wastrels. And here—this is important too—is how one dresses the bottle with the bag." Carefully removing a bottle of MD 20/20, Der Platoniker twisted the paper around the short neck of the bottle until the cap was exposed. "See how neatly the brown bag covers the name of this pernicious liquid—thereby protecting it from the prying eyes of children or the inadvertent gaze of people of good breeding—but leaving the spout exposed for the delectation of the deadbeat imbiber?"

"Uh—yeah! That's kinda cool! If y'all don't mind me asking, um, where're y'all gonna go drink this stuff?"

"In fact, we *do* mind," injected Schwanzie. "It's a trade secret. We tell you, you tell your mother, who tells your great-uncle Harry and before you know it, all of the good doorways are gone! And as for the park benches—well!"

"Well!" added Der Platoniker, nodding vigorously.

"Hey, man, I'm sorry, um...I didn't know about...all that. You guys have a good evening."

Schwanzie and Der Platoniker left the convenience store, barely able to keep straight faces. The attendant's mouth was still hanging open in bafflement as he picked his nose.

The two retirees howled with laughter as they drove away. "Ya know, Platoniker, we could take this act on the road! Travel around the country visiting convenience stores and buying cheap rotgut while being filmed by hidden cameras. Ha!"

"What I'd love to have on camera is The Juice's face Saturday night when he starts doling out glasses of putrid plonk!"

"'Research has clearly proven...' How'd you come up with that?" asked Schwanzie.

"Same way you came up with the brown bag etiquette! That poor kid is probably googling his brain out trying to find out about all of this!"

"Yeah, if he hasn't picked his brain out through his nose!" Schwanzie eased his car off the road into the relative calm of The Woods, but came to a dead stop in front of the admin building.

"Something the matter?" queried Der Platoniker.

"Not at all. It was something you said—about filming The Juice's face at the wine-tasting. How utterly simple!" Schwanzie slapped the steering wheel as he laughed to himself.

"What?"

"The wine-tasting will be easy to film! Everybody has a camera in their pockets these days—their phones. And most of our fellow residents are on Facebook with their children and grandkids. It'll be the greatest gag ever. We won't just record The Juice's face—we'll record everybody's faces as they taste bastardized wines! It will go viral on the Internet!"

"The Juice might even have to emigrate!"

A gentle toot on a car horn reminded the conspirators they were blocking the road. Schwanzie gave a little wave of apology and rolled to the parking area in front of his apartment. The bottles were clinking as they made their way to the front door, giggling like schoolboys.

When Schwanzie opened the apartment door, Twilight was sitting on the sofa, wearing her bra over her blouse, listening to Benny Goodman and swaying to the music. When she saw her husband and Der Platoniker, Twilight smiled and said, "Oh, I see you've brought a friend home!" Putting on her glasses she added, "Oh, it's The Plonker! How nice."

"Platoniker, Twilight sweetie, it's Der Platoniker." Schwanzie went over and gently kissed his wife on the forehead. "And now, *schatzie*, he and I have work to do!"

Seven

The Kids Call In: Keska Saye

There was a somber mood as Keska's two adult children, Alain
and Marie, along with their spouses, arrived this grey Saturday
morning. In fact, Alain's wife, Corinne, had offered to stay outside
with the three grandchildren in a play area as Alain and Marie were
returning the ashes of Keska's deceased husband, their father, Mark.
Keska was floating gaily about her apartment preparing coffee and
tea for her family. The three other adults looked at one another nervously, having internal doubts as to whether Keska remembered why
they had come. Alain nervously fingered the bag which contained the
box of ashes he had collected from the nearby university hospital,
to which his father had left his mortal remains for research purpos-
es four months previously. His sister, Marie, decided to try to get
their mother to sit for what she—and the others—assumed would be
a matter of some gravity. Instead, Keska swept her daughter into her

vortex and soon had her carrying cake out to the coffee table. She rolled her eyes at her brother.

"There," smiled Keska, pleased with her hospitality. "Alain dear, wouldn't you like to invite Corinne and the children in for cake and tea?"

"Yeah, well, about that, *Maman.*" Alain and Marie had always used the French term to address their mother.

"Oh Alain, do call me Keska Saye like everyone else here at The Woods. *Maman* seems so *passé.*"

Drawing in a deep breath, Alain responded, "Why don't you sit down, Keska? We think it's best to leave the children outside for the moment."

"Well, if you insist, then I shall."

"Yes, please," added Marie.

"Really, I can't see what all of the fuss is about. It's not as if any of you has died."

"It's about Papa," spoke Marie.

"Well, he's dead already," chirped Keska, "So there's no reason to be so glum."

"*Ma-*...um...Keska, we *know* our father is dead. That's kinda the reason we're here, remember? We told you that the hospital had called and said Papa's remains had been cremated and were ready to be picked up. So that's what we have done...and they're here." Alain lifted the bag, as if he needed proof.

To the surprise of all, Keska burst out laughing, and was then joined by Marie's husband, Ralph. It was then that Marie noticed the bag Alain into which had put the box. It bore the likeness of Colonel Sanders and the motto "Finger lickin' good."

"Alain, *really*? That was the only bag you could find?"

By then, Keska had covered her face as she was laughing so hard. "I sent Mike to the utility room to fetch a large plastic bag...they're all wadded up in a drawer," Alain replied dejectedly. "I didn't know..."

"How delightful!" Keska clapped her hands. "Don't be so hard on your brother, Marie. You've always placed too much emphasis on being the older sibling. What do the younger people say these days? Chill up!"

"Chill out," Marie glumly replied.

"Yes, that too," chided her mother. Then turning back to Alain, Keska said, "Well, dear, pass him over."

Alain stood, walked over to his mother and handed her the bag. He helped her as she lifted out the box containing her late husband's ashes. Setting the box on a side table, she turned to the others and said, "I've never actually seen anyone's ashes before. Have you?"

All averred that they had not. "Well, come on then!" Keska beckoned the other three to join her as she gingerly lifted the lid from the box. They were all silent for about ten seconds and then Keska spoke. "Well, Mark, there you are...Remember that blow job I promised you?" and with that Keska blew at the ashes, sending a plume over all four of them.

Marie uttered a cry of horror, Ralph sneezed and Alain blurted, "Jesus Christ, Mother!"

Keska let loose a laugh straight from the gut. She laughed even harder as the other three frantically tried to rid themselves of the ashes—as though death were contagious. "Oh, you should just see yourselves!" Marie was brushing her hair; Ralph was wiping his face with his handkerchief and Alain was using a napkin to remove his father's dust.

"Couldn't you just show a little dignity, *Maman*?" Marie chided. Then, indicating the ashes, she added, "I mean, after all it...they... um...*he* was your husband of over forty years, and our father."

Keska nodded as though agreeing and then blew hard at the ashes again. Alain exploded, "Aw for fuck's sake, Mother!"

Keska feigned shock and then asked, "Well, what naughty boy isn't going to be allowed cake?"

"As though I'd eat it now with...with Papa's ashes all over it." Marie nodded in agreement, while Ralph simply sat there stupefied.

"Oh, just think of it as your father being icing on the cake!" coaxed Keska, cutting a large piece of cake. "Here, Alain, have a piece of your father." Ralph looked as grey as the ashes and said he thought he was going to be sick.

"Well, you know where the bathroom is," giggled Keska. "Honestly, why are you all so squeamish? Your father spread himself around when he was alive, so why shouldn't we do the same with him now?"

"What do you mean by that, *Maman*?" queried Marie.

"*Alors chèrie*, are you pretending not to know or are you actually that ignorant of your father's infidelities?"

"Papa's *infidelities*?"

"Oh dear, I didn't think people your age were so naïve these days. Why do you think so many female students needed extra tuition—in the evenings? Some even came to the house—the poor things really thought I couldn't see what was written in their eyes and the way they fawned around Mark. It's a wonder some of them didn't orgasm when he simply brushed by them."

"Are you serious?" gasped Marie.

"*Maman*, this really is too much. This is our father you're talking about," added Alain.

"Don't worry, Alain, he can't hear me. He's dead, remember?"

"Yes, but..."

"But what, dear boy? Are you one of those who feel that death somehow bestows dignity on those who hadn't earned it in life?" Alain sat as though posing for a portrait, every muscle frozen.

"*Maman*," interjected Marie, "even if this were so—"

"And it is," asserted Keska.

"Even *if it were so*," reiterated Marie, "then why didn't you divorce Father? Why tell us all of this now?"

"Oh...*que dire*?" Keska began. "You and your brother so adored your father—as did I. And well...to be quite truthful, I found ways of satisfying my needs. Just not so blatantly as your father. And I still do today; I'm not dead you know."

"Good God, *Maman*, are you saying you have a lover?"

"Why only *one*, dear boy?" Keska winked at Alain whose mouth dropped open like a ventriloquist's dummy. "Really, my children, fretting about sex-talk at your ages? I assume your children are not the products of immaculate conception? Do you think your mother is not attractive to men, or has no needs of her own?"

Alain was virtually squirming in his seat. "But you're our mother, for heaven's sake."

Keska giggled. "What happened to 'fuck's sake' now that we speak of sex?" She threw her head back and laughed at the ceiling. "This is sooo amusing!"

"Maybe for you, *Mother*," snapped Marie.

"Oh Marie—and Alain—I do love you so. You so amuse me! Marie, did you think I never found the dildo you hid under your mattress? Or your sex magazines, Alain? Of course, I knew you were masturbating. It's part of life and growing up. Oh, dear, you are both blushing! How sweet!"

Ashen, Ralph stood up woodenly and said, "I-I'm gonna go out and see the kids."

"Thanks a lot, husband-mine," grumbled Marie.

"So, *Maman*, are you going to tell us who your new boyfriend is?"

"He's not my boyfriend—he's married—he is simply my lover."

"Now wait a minute!" barked Marie. "Are you telling us you're having an affair with a married man, in a small community like this? What does his wife have to say about it?"

"Oh nothing, really. Twilight is in her own happy world—and Schwanzie, her husband, takes very good care of her...and of me, too!" Keska giggled.

"Schwanzie!?" snarled Alain. "What kind of name is that? It sounds Yiddish."

"What's in any name, dear? But his name *is* descriptive, for he has the most marvellous *schwanz*, of which he is justly proud." Keska used her hands to indicate the length.

Fingers outspread, Alain was waving both hands as though trying to rub out the image his mother had just described. But to no avail, of course, as the image was firmly planted in his brain. "Oh, gawd, Mother! A Yiddish gigolo! That's just...wonderful!"

Marie had stood and was frantically walking back and forth, running her hands through her hair. "I can't believe what I'm hearing—and you of all people!"

"Oh Marie, it's not *just me*, darling. Schwanzie is having sex with any number of the women here. He is so thoughtful that way."

"I'll just bet he is," growled Marie. Alain was holding his head in his hands, mumbling something unintelligible.

"You should just see him—it's all so dramatic *and romantic*! He wears a cape and a mask—not unlike Zorro—and these *very tight* leggings—ou-lah!" Keska's eyes rolled back dreamily. Then she perked up as an idea was hatched. Turning to Marie, she asked, "Perhaps you'd like to try him? I can arrange it."

Alain joined his sister in treading the floor. Both were making exclamations, more to themselves than to Keska, who watched her adult children bemusedly. And then, as though their actions had been choreographed, the siblings stopped and turned to their mother, each trying to speak over the other.

Keska gently waved her hands and said, "*Doucement, mes enfants*. Gently and one at a time." She then pointed to Marie.

"Y-you're having group sex here at Carolina Woods?!"

"Nothing of the sort, *chèrie*. No, Schwanzie visits us discreetly—and discretely!" Keska was delighted with her pun.

"And safe sex, *Maman*?" interjected Alain. "I hope you are using protection?"

"You must be joking, Alain. It's not as though any of us can get pregnant at our age!"

"Th-that's not what I meant! I mean AIDS!"

"Oh darling, we have no use for sex aids. We simply enjoy ourselves as we are."

Alain thrust out his hand dramatically, in silent film style. "That's it! That's *IT*! I'm outta here! This whole place is a nuthouse." Swinging the door open, Alain paused and looked at his sister. "Are you coming or staying?"

Totally flummoxed, Marie tried to speak. "I...uh...well...um." Then she kissed her mother's hand, patted her on the head and left.

Outside, the parents were trying to round up their children while trying to explain why they were leaving. In the confusion, Keska appeared at the door, bearing her cake. "Don't you want to take this with you? I made it for you and the children."

Children squealed from the cars; then car tires squealed as her offspring sped away. Taking the cake back into her apartment, Keska sat down by the coffee table. She picked up the piece of cake she had cut for Alain and, cutting into it, enjoyed a mouthful. Remembering the box of ashes, she reached over and patted them. "Well Mark, here we are again...just the two of us."

Eight

The Vine's Vengeance

Twilight, Schwanzie, Keys, Keska Saye and others—even Great White—had gathered in Der Platoniker's little cottage. Each of them had a vessel of some sort in which to decant the wines to be imbibed that evening at The Juice's much-vaunted wine-tasting. Both Keska and Der Platoniker had sauntered through the dining hall to count how many bottles would need to be half-drained. They also tipped the evening staff very handsomely to turn a blind eye to this evening's shenanigans. The ladies' handbags and men's overcoats held the various bottles of MD 20/20, Thunderbird and other insults to a wine connoisseur's palate. Schwanzie and Der Platoniker had had the foresight to purchase a dozen funnels to make their tasks flow more smoothly. Each member of the conspiracy was provided with a wad of paper towels with which to mop up any mess that might serve to tip off The Juice.

The team was pumped and ready. Only one thing remained: the telephone call to the main building, which would necessitate The Juice's return to his apartment. As Schwanzie had a New York accent, it was agreed that he would call the reception desk, pretending to be a relative of The Juice, and thereby lure him away from his presentation table and back to his abode. When the clock showed ten-past-seven, Der Platoniker called reception. At the same time, the saboteurs exited the cottage and began making their way to the wine-tasting. About halfway there, they were met by a flush-faced Juice, huffing and puffing his way back to a 'very important call.' Cheered by the number of participants he met going toward the main building, he breathlessly called out, "Not to worry! I'll be with you shortly."

"Take your time!" replied Schwanzie. "We're in no rush." But as soon as The Juice was out of sight, they all moved as quickly as their aging bodies would allow. Soon they were at it. Marvin Hendricks and Richard Wilson were on hand this evening to assist the residents in any way. The tips had sealed their lips, but piqued their curiosity. When they saw a gang of elderly white folk pulling out bottles of cheap wine, as well as funnels and empty bottles, they could stand by no longer.

"Let me help you with that," said Richard to Twilight as she fumbled with a screw-on top. "Mmh-mmh, the Mad Dog," Richard shook his head. "Brings back memories of some *baaad* hangovers." Twilight smiled at her helper.

Marvin dashed into the kitchen and brought out some carafes, to make the task quicker. "I'll keep the good stuff in here. Just catch me after the gig!"

Within ten minutes, their work was complete. Six bottles of red wine stood like sentinels along the linen tablecloth, with their six companion bottles of white in their chillers; two of each type. The co-conspirators spread themselves out among the table and chairs, greeting their fellow residents as they took their seats in readiness for the evening's event. Baskets of French bread adorned each table, for palate cleaning. They were accompanied by tubs for spitting or emptying un-drunk wines and fresh water for rinsing glasses. About fourteen other members of the community joined the wine saboteurs. Most had never attended one of The Juice's performances, but a few were the sort who would attend every event, no matter what.

Der Platoniker joined Schwanzie and Twilight at their table. Twilight was wearing a petticoat over her trousers, with pink fluffy slippers on her feet. Given the time, her eyes were already beginning to glaze over. Schwanzie leaned toward her ear and whispered, "*Nu?* You want to miss the fun? And after you got all gussied up?" Twilight smiled lovingly at her husband and even managed to perk up.

The Juice was several minutes behind time when he rushed into the dining hall, looking somewhat befuddled. He mumbled something about having had an important phone call and then glanced about the room as though to make sure everything was just as he had left it, while running his hand over his thinning white hair. His smile not only seemed forced; it positively appeared as though someone had shoved a live electric cable up his backside. One of the residents asked whether The Juice would mind if they recorded the session to share with their families. Flattered at the thought—and the exposure (what if it went viral on the Internet?)—he magnanimously agreed. Smartphones were duly set up to record the affair.

Next followed The Juice's little rituals that always preceded his uttering of words. Namely, he smacked his lips, breathed in deeply through his flaring nostrils and raised his right hand as though swearing an oath or trying to silence a noisy gathering—neither of which obtained in this case. His countenance bespoke an attitude of 'you have no idea what pearls I am about to cast before you swine.' Someone blurted out "Just get on with it!" A ripple of sniggers ran through the audience. The Juice ran through his rituals again, smiled painfully and began.

"Now, I know there are three things that everyone thinks he or she possesses: a sense of humor, a good judge of character and knowledge of decent wine." More lip-smacking, raising of hand and nostril breathing.

A muffled voice called out, "Enlighten us, oh wizard of wine!" Another eruption of nervous sniggers. Those for whom this was their first tasting with The Juice showed their annoyance and looked for the culprit. But as at least three-quarters of those in attendance were hard of hearing, no one could be quite sure from where the voice originated.

The Juice pontificated on the rise, fall, and rebound of the fruit of the vine in America, lingering in dolorous tones over Prohibition, and then taking his audience on a cross-country tour from the Sonoma Valley to their very own local vineyards in central North Carolina. Then The Juice went in for the kill, as he let his auditors know why they really didn't like the wines they thought they liked and had served at home for years. (Yes, dear Reader, The Juice *is* a *wine snob*—and insufferable with it. Honestly, you must have encountered at least one by now.) The few attendees who actually knew a little about wine felt suitably chastised and anticipated being liberated from their untutored palates. But The Juice was far from finished with dashing their joy in a Kendall Jackson Chardonnay or a West Bend Grenache. His was a search and destroy mission, intended to leave the audience as subservient putty in his hands. Lips were again smacked, deep breathing through his ruddy alcoholic's nose and the hand moving upward as though beyond his control. The Juice told his audience about 'nose,' 'body,' 'legs,' at which a wit erupted, "Are you describing your dog or wine?" The Juice's mouth hung open as he scanned the faces, searching for a give-away smirk. None was found. The Juice's hair was rubbed, lips smacked, breath taken through flared nostrils, hand raised and mouth opened for his peroration and then a voice shouted, "Hey, *oinos interruptus*, just pour the goddamn wine!"

The Juice's arm fell with a slap against his thigh. He glared at the audience with mixed alarm and distress, as if they were a lynch mob. Having forgotten his prepared speech, The Juice decided to end his verbal offensive and start pouring. The wine selections this evening would all be from American vineyards. The silence in the room was palpable as The Juice brought the first bottle of red to each table, solemnly pouring the shiny liquid into each glass. He invited them to swirl the wine in the glass and notice the 'legs' on the inside of the glass as the wine settled. Then he encouraged the group to enjoy the bouquet, at which point he lifted his glass to his nose. The Juice's eyes widened in consternation, but undeterred, he adjured everyone to taste this magnificent liquid. Only two or three managed to keep the wine in their mouths. Most—including The Juice—reflexively spat it back into the glass, while one of the saboteurs announced, "Mmh, Château de Pisspot, I believe!" The Juice made a weak attempt at laughter and announced that the wine must be 'corked.' Another of his tormentors piped up, "Of course it was corked; we saw you remove them earlier."

The Juice was now on the ropes and began a feeble attempt to explain 'corked' in wine terminology. But for once, he managed to stop himself and instead asked everyone—except for the few who had drained their glasses—to pour the wretched liquid into the receptacles provided and rinse their glasses in the tubs of water. Now that only one bottle of this particular red was left, The Juice explained that he would only be able to share a small amount with each person. Around the tables he went, sparely dribbling the wine into the waiting glasses. With confidence, The Juice repeated his instructions, but this time joined in with the group giving a satisfied smile as he placed his purple proboscis in the glass. His face began twitching and his eyes widened in disgust as the olfactory nerves registered alarm signals. Grunts, ughs and oh-nos echoed around the room.

The Juice hurriedly dumped the contents of his glass, and urged others to follow suit. Clearing his throat, he croaked, "Let's try a white next. Clearly, that case of red has experienced some sort of contamination." Having rinsed their glasses, The Juice praised the Chambourcin they were about to experience. As though to make up for the previous train crash of a wine-tasting, he went among the tables with a bottle in each hand, pouring generous amounts and praising the French/American hybrid. Glasses were swirled, legs were sought—in vain—and the contents entered expectant mouths...

"*Merde alors!*" It was Keska Saye who had blurted out in her native tongue.

"Why have you brought us here?" cried Schwanzie, "To poison us?"

Then, to everyone's surprise, Twilight's sweet little voice shrieked, "Brucify him!" And with that, she threw a piece of bread at The Juice. Without hesitation, others took up the cry, "Brucify him! Brucify him!" The dining hall erupted like a college food fight. Pieces of bread began flying at Bruce The Juice. An atmosphere of pandemonium ensued as people filled their glasses with the undrinkable admixtures and drenched The Juice. Marvin and Richard were doubled over with laughter, unable to intervene as they watched the seniors behave like adolescents at a frat party. A few of the attendees were checking out the untouched bottles to see whether or not there was anything worth imbibing. If not, it went on The Juice. (Reader, haven't you ever wanted to see an outcome like this?)

The Juice, trying to retain whatever dignity he had left within him, turned on his heel and walked out of the dining room. "Don't forget to spit!" Schwanzie called after him. Peals of laughter followed. Several of the wine saboteurs set to putting their videos online, while the others began the task of cleaning up. Marvin and Richard, over their hysterics, lent a hand.

Marvin encouraged the workers by asking, "Would anyone care to partake of the *real* wine?" He went into the kitchen and came out with carafes and jugs of the various wines, which he placed on The Juice's front table. "Be my—or should I say, The Juice's—guests!" Glasses were filled as the raucous retirees sought to make the dining room acceptable for tomorrow's breakfast. Having allowed their 'wards' to make the mess, Richard and Marvin put their elbow grease fervently into the job at hand.

Richard paused thoughtfully for a moment, leaning on his mop, and said, "You know, I used to worry about getting older, but since I came to work here—and watching y'all tonight. I think I'm really gonna enjoy it!" His words were met with acclamations of "Hear, hear!" and the clinking of glasses.

Nine

The Introductory Sermon

Jimmy T was in the auditorium bright and early for his first service at The Woods. Keys pitched up a few minutes later, as she would play piano for the hymns, wearing a dress which was extremely *décolleté* for Sunday service. Jimmy couldn't help but notice the septuagenarian's ample cleavage and inwardly reprimanded himself for letting his gaze linger too long. *She's old enough to be your grandmother!* Knowing that most of the congregation would be nearly two generations older than he, Jimmy had brought a couple of older hymnals. His idea was to request hymns from those in attendance and then, with his smartphone, he would photograph the lyrics and run them through the projector onto the screen over the stage. Schwanzie and Der Platoniker had volunteered to operate the projector for the service. These two arch-conspirators from the previous evening's derailed wine-tasting were still giggling over their success and reviewing the videos on their phones.

A larger-than-usual congregation made an appearance to hear the student chaplain's first service. Some carried large cards with them and sat together near the back. Jimmy heard guffaws of laughter from some of those entering for the service. He was not to know they were re-hashing Saturday night's events. In any case, Jimmy greeted the beaming faces with his own, walking forward with outstretched hand to introduce himself to his new flock. Several were disappointed that he had not worn the jacket with **Chaplin** on it—after their first encounter, Schwanzie had wasted no time in merrily spreading the word. And they had so looked forward to using their Charlie Chaplin jokes. Nevertheless, there were lots of whispers as people debated whether or not Jimmy T looked like Jim Bakker.

Once nearly all of the congregation had gathered—there were always stragglers using canes and walking frames—Jimmy announced, "Let us pray!" He entreated the Almighty for blessings on the service and the people, and prayed that God would make himself known to all of them today. Jimmy then asked if there might be a hymn folks would like to sing. There were shrugs and murmurs while Jimmy waited.

Behind him, Keys popped up, "How about 'Begin the Beguine'?"

Taken by surprise, Jimmy hurriedly interjected that he didn't seem to have that one in his hymnals. Happily, he had marked a few in case there were no suggestions. He reached for his mobile phone only to realize it wasn't in its normal place in his right jacket pocket. Trying to act nonchalant, Jimmy began patting all of his pockets—jacket (inside and out) and then his trousers. One of the residents called out, "Oh, I do like this game!" and started singing "Head, Shoulders, Knees and Toes." One or two others joined in. The Card Crew held up numbers ranging from 5 to 10. Jimmy had been awarded an average of 8.

Jimmy was blushing various shades of the red spectrum. He waved his hands to regain silence and stated that he had forgotten his phone.

"Did you want to call someone, sweetie? I think I have mine here...somewhere." An old dear began searching her handbag for her phone—as did several others.

"No!" groaned Jimmy T. "I don't want to call anyone. I just wanted to take a picture of the hymns so we could project them onto the screen." He pointed toward the blank screen. There were nods and noises which indicated, "Now we understand." Jimmy looked disconcertedly as the Card Crew gave him an average of 4.

From the rear, Schwanzie shouted, "Here, use mine!" and walked forward, extending his mobile.

Remembering their first encounter, Jimmy blurted, "I thought you were Jewish."

"Not 'were,' still am! I went to *shul* yesterday, so today I give you a chance. Remember, Jesus was ours before you guys got hold of him. Let's just say I'm open to hearing what you have to say."

While Jimmy snapped a few photos of hymns, Schwanzie sidled over to Keys admiringly and whispered something in her ear. She stifled a laugh while nodding at him. Jimmy coughed to get Schwanzie's attention and handed the phone back to him. Schwanzie returned to the projector and plugged his phone into the USB port. Jimmy looked back at Der Platoniker and Schwanzie and was given the thumbs up.

Raising his hands heavenwards, Jimmy enthusiastically proclaimed, "Let us praise the Lord!"

Keys started playing the tune to "Blessed Assurance" while the screen was filled with images from the previous night and the loudspeakers carried the sound: The Juice's contorted face—along with those of others—as the rancid wine was tasted, the cries of 'Brucify him!,' the pelting of bread and the dousing of wine. Ripples of laughter played across the congregation. Jimmy stepped forward to get a look at what was on the screen. Meanwhile those who had not attended The Juice's wine-tasting looked on with amused curiosity; while those who had been there pointed out their favorite parts, shouting out, "Just look at The Juice!" or "See the look on your face!"

Keys, undeterred, continued banging out "Blessed Assurance." Jimmy's head tilted to one side as he tried to make sense of older adults throwing bread and wine at a tall man who stood with a shocked expression. The Card Crew were all waving 10s.

"W-what is this?!" Jimmy shouted above the hubbub. Squinting at the amateur video, he asked in amazement, "Isn't that some of y'all?" He looked accusingly at faces in the congregation. "What did y'all do to that poor man? Is this some kind of joke or what?" Jimmy was totally nonplussed. "We're supposed to be worshiping—or at least that's what I thought."

"Sorry about that, Chaplain," Schwanzie's voice came from the rear of the hall. "I'm not too savvy about mobile technology and simply clicked on the wrong file. It won't happen again." A few voices emitted an 'Awww' of disappointment. Meanwhile Keys was still playing "Blessed Assurance." Jimmy turned toward her, calling, "Miss!? Ma'am?!" Keys was so absorbed with her playing—and humming along to the tune—that she never heard him...until he shouted, "Cut it out!"

Keys stopped mid-tune and the whole place went silent. When Keys saw the look on Jimmy's face, she burst into tears. Schwanzie bellowed, "Now look what you've done! You schmuck!" Schwanzie marched forward to comfort Keys, who buried her face into his chest. Heads were shaken in disapproval and many a 'tut-tut' was heard. Jimmy turned in every direction, as though searching for support from his alienated flock.

"Look y'all, I'm really sorry...but, you know...I...er...I didn't know what was going on." By then, Jimmy was sweating profusely. He ran his index finger around his collar, then loosened his tie. He tried to smile, but the muscles refused to obey his mental command.

One of the ladies in the congregation spoke up. "Say, he does look like Jim Bakker, doesn't he?" Everyone turned to his or her neighbor to discuss the likeness, as Jimmy stood in bewilderment. He even feared he might start crying.

As Schwanzie led Keys out of the auditorium, he shot a fierce glare at Jimmy. The chaplain sensed someone approaching him from his blind side and turned to see Rocky. Before Jimmy could speak, Rocky said, "You little creep. Somebody oughta punch you right in da mouth...*me!*" Rocky's fist made acquaintance with the chaplain's nose. As Jimmy toppled to the floor, the oldsters with the number cards gave a standing ovation and—you guessed it—another perfect ten.

Ten

The Introductory Sermon Debrief

"I-I honestly don't know what happened." Jimmy T was wringing his hands together and looking at his knees. When he looked up at Gretchen Beauxreves, his swollen upper lip and purplish nose—from Rocky's ministrations—made him look vaguely like a duck. Gretchen bit her lower lip to keep from smiling. "I mean, I was...like trying to get worship started and then this weird video appeared on the screen instead of the hymn we were supposed to sing and in the video people were...um...like throwing bread and wine all over a man and—"

"Sounds like a bizarre way to share the Eucharist," interrupted Gretchen. "Was this meant to be a part of your service?"

"No, heavens no!" protested Jimmy. "Oh—was that meant to be a joke?"

"Maybe." Gretchen shrugged.

"Well, in the video I noticed that some of the folks who were in the worship service were there!"

"There *where*?"

"A-at the wine and bread throwing, um...thing."

"Jimmy, I'm really sorry, but I haven't a clue what you're talking about."

Becoming more frustrated, Jimmy got to his feet and started pacing. "When the weird video started playing, a lot of those at the Sunday service were talking about it happening the night before—um, Saturday night."

"The night before Saturday night? Do you mean Friday night?"

"No!" Jimmy barked.

Gretchen straightened up and said, "Mind your tone of voice, Mr. Watkins."

"I'm sorry, Ms. Beauxreves, I meant Saturday night—the night before—"

"Sunday morning, I understand. Just try to calm down, okay?"

"I'm just so upset about the way things went."

"Clearly."

Stopping in mid-pace, Jimmy appeared to have a revelation. "You know, Ms. Beauxreves, people here seem to do some really funny things. Have you noticed?"

"Funny 'ha-ha' or funny strange?"

"Strange!" emphasized Jimmy.

"Can't really say I have noticed. Would you care to elaborate?"

"Well, you've seen my face, haven't you?"

"Ah yes, I admit that it is a bit strange—looking like Jim Bakker. Is that what you meant?"

"No, I mean..." Jimmy's hand wobbled around as he embarrassedly pointed toward his fat lip and bruised nose. "This! One of the residents slugged me yesterday—a guy called Rocky."

"Really, Jimmy, getting into a fight with a resident—and on your first Sunday—is very unfortunate. And to engage in violence with someone old enough to be your grandfather—honestly. Have you apologized?"

"Me apologize? He slugged me! All I did was tell the piano player lady to stop playing the hymn over and over while the video was on!" Being a Southern Baptist male, taking instructions from a woman was almost more than Jimmy could bear. But he knew he had to get through this field education. He must complete his seminary training and be ordained. There were so many souls to convert to the intolerance known as evangelicalism, so many things from which people must be saved: women's rights, Democrats, progressive views about sexuality—and all of the alphabet-soup-LGBT-whatever that went with it! And then there were issues such as Jews, Muslims, Hindus, Catholics—and liberal Christians—all peoples of questionable faiths. His mind was already on a crusade.

"Jimmy?"

"Uh...yes, ma'am?"

"So, you were saying you wanted the piano playing to stop because you wanted to watch the video? Yet I thought I heard you say it was 'weird.' Do you have a taste for the bizarre?"

"No! No!" Jimmy was almost stamping his feet in frustration. "The video got everybody's attention. I only looked at it to see what the heck was going on. They were all laughing and talking about this guy named The Juice and what they had done to him and...and when I tried to get everybody to stop talking and laughing...well, the woman playing the piano just kept playing and—"

Gretchen interrupted, "But I thought you wanted her to play. Wasn't that the case?"

"No—I mean *yes*, I had wanted her to play...but...um just not..." Jimmy's voice trailed off as he looked at the ceiling, perhaps appealing for divine aid.

"Jimmy, please sit. Here, have a glass of water." Gretchen poured water from a jug which sat on her desk. Jimmy took the glass, had a sip and then started to speak again.

"No, just drink it all—but slowly—and take some deep breaths along the way. Let's see if we can bring some clarity to all of this."

Gulp. Breath. Gulp. Breath. Jimmy tried to regain his composure. The devil was surely at work in this woman. He must remain in control and be watchful of her wiles.

Gretchen tried to recap: "So, you wanted music and got it. Then you wanted the music to stop because the video came on. Am I right so far?" Jimmy nodded in agreement. "Okay, because the video was running and the lady, who I assume was Keys, kept playing a hymn, you did what?"

"I just asked her to stop." The chaplain turned his hands palm-upward as though to say, "Innocent little me."

"And that started a fight?" Gretchen fixed her gaze on Jimmy, whose eyes darted about.

"Well, she sorta started crying."

"She 'sorta' cried or she cried—please be specific."

"Um...she really cried." Jimmy wiggled his jaw nervously and ran his finger around his collar as he became more nervous. "I kinda had to...um, raise my voice...sorta."

"Might we use the word 'shout'?" queried Gretchen.

"Yeah, yeah, I guess you could say that, but you see there was the video noise and all of the people talking and laughing and I couldn't get Keys to stop, so I sorta shouted to 'cut it out'."

"And then you engaged in a punch-up?"

"Yeah—no!—well, I mean I was the one who got punched! I hadn't done a thing—"

"Except shout at a sweet, delightful older lady and cause her to cry. What happened to pastoral concern?"

"Well, they were all acting like a bunch of loonies!" blurted Jimmy. He raised his hand and waved it as though trying to catch his words, all the while realizing he was digging his hole deeper and deeper. "Anyway, this guy comes up and punches me on the nose and mouth." Jimmy pointed at the aggrieved area, wincing as he accidentally touched his nose. "It bled." Gretchen said nothing but kept looking at Jimmy. And, yes, he was one of those people who has to fill a silence with words. "Uh—this Jewish guy came up first and called me a...uh...schmuck or something. And I don't even know why he was there in the first place." Jimmy nodded as though that final thought made his case.

"You've lived a sheltered life, haven't you?"

"Um...not really, I get about—and I worked for the fire depart-ment—don't forget."

"How could I?" smiled Gretchen. "What I meant was, you haven't spent much time around people who aren't like you, have you? People from other parts of the country or other parts of the world, for that matter."

"No...I guess not." Jimmy felt and looked like a whipped pup. The devil-woman had beaten him.

"Look, Jimmy, we're all allowed mistakes. But I want you to go and apologize to Rocky. He's very protective of his fellow residents. Understood?" Jimmy nodded. "*Today.*" The young chaplain's eyes widened, but the look he received from his supervisor said, "Not another word." Jimmy turned toward the door, but was stopped by Gretchen. "And Keys as well—you mustn't forget her." The chaplain nodded his already drooping head and was gone.

Eleven

The Juice Seeps Out

After his public embarrassment, The Juice thought he could emerge after a few days of seclusion. He had enough food in the fridge—and just enough wine to keep him nearly embalmed while the more egregious effects of his version of a "Saturday Night Massacre" wore off. But then it happened: his children and grandchildren got in touch via Facebook over the most hilarious viral video they had ever seen and—you guessed it—it was his Brucifixion.

His elder son, Bruce Jr., wrote: "Didn't realize you guys were engaging in bacchanalias there at The Woods. I loved the way you stood stock-still through the whole prank. Did you think it up or did you have help? No matter. Wish I had seen this side of you when I was growing up! Good going, Dad!"

Bruce Jr's son, Brice—his father thought it more clever than Bruce the Third, so combined Bruce with thrice and...well you get the picture—was fourteen and still a newbie on Facebook, but he had compiled all of the videos of his grandfather which had been posted on the Internet and sent them to The Juice with the comment, "You rock, Gramps!" The Juice returned their compliments with non-committal remarks. He had simply wanted to forget the whole damned affair—but now his humiliation was everywhere! How to escape his confinement and restock his limited supplies of food, and more importantly, drink?

The Juice had lost his driver's license for getting behind the wheel once too often, both under the influence and without wearing a seatbelt. Though it was something of a nuisance to him, the upside was that he could drink whenever he wanted and however much he wanted. Besides, The Woods regularly ran a shuttle bus to the major supermarkets, but they didn't go out after nine p.m. The Juice would have preferred shopping after ten o'clock at night, when there would be much less likelihood that he'd be seen or recognized by anyone from The Woods, but it was still mid-afternoon and he was hungry. And of course, to use the shuttle bus would be social suicide. That left only the nearby convenience store—ironically the self-same store from which Schwanzie and Der Platoniker had bought the cheap wine. The Juice had never been one for exercise, so the half-mile walk to the store was anathema—it would also have meant he had to cross the grounds, pass in front of the administration building and walk along the busy road which ran past The Woods. Thus, he did the only thing left to him: he called a taxi. It could park directly in front of his apartment building, which meant minimum exposure. The Juice felt the first sense of relief in days.

Wearing a trench coat, hat and sunglasses—despite it being a cloudy day—The Juice waited for the taxi's horn. When it sounded, he dashed out his door, avoided the elevator and took the stairs down to the emergency exit. From there it was twenty yards to his waiting ride. He flopped back in the seat as the taxi pulled away.

"Where to, *amigo?*" The Juice was relieved to hear the Hispanic accent of his driver. Bruce told the driver that he only needed to go to the local convenience store. The driver looked at him curiously. "Hey man, if you don't mind me saying, you coulda walked there." Bruce grumbled under his breath, but the friendly driver was undeterred. As they drove past the entrance, the driver exclaimed, "Hey, now I know why this place sounded familiar! You guys are the old folks who threw that wild party! I seen it on Facebook! Man, you guys have some wild parties here, right?" The Juice slipped lower in his seat. The taxi pulled into the parking area beside the store.

"Wait here, if you don't mind. I'll pay you for the time." The Juice struggled to pull his long frame out of the car. In doing so, he knocked off his hat and his sunglasses. As he stooped to pick them up, his face was almost level with the driver's—whose eyes widened with recognition. The driver switched off the engine and got out of his cab.

"Hey man, you're that dude! I knew there was something familiar about you!" He followed The Juice into the store. The nose-picker was sitting at the cash register doing what he was best at. He acknowledged the taxi driver.

"Hey, Rafael, what's happenin'?"

"Yo, Ronnie, look at this." (Yes, the nose-picker has a name.) Rafael shoved his cell phone under Ronnie's over-exercised nose. "Get a load of this—he's the guy!" He pointed at the video and then at The Juice.

This proved to be the highlight of Ronnie's young life. "No way, man! Really?"

"Really, dude! I picked him up at that old folk's place down the road." Keeping an eye on The Juice, who was even more visible with his hat, Rafael exclaimed, "And I'm giving him a ride back there! I gotta get a selfie with him!"

The slow-moving gears in Ronnie's brain began to turn. "Wait a minute! There was a coupla old guys in here last week and they was buying really cheap wine. But they didn't look—or smell—like your normal winos. They was laughin' and jokin' about something they was gonna do...show me that video clip again."

Rafael complied, handing his phone to Ronnie. "Yeah! Yeah, dude!" He showed the frozen image to Rafael. "These're the guys that bought the wine! Man, they're like celebrities! Let's both get some selfies with 'im!"

Meanwhile, The Juice was glancing nervously at the excited conversation between the two young men. At six-foot-five, and wearing a hat, he could hardly take refuge behind the shelving. Being recognized by a taxi driver—of all things! He couldn't buy enough food in this store to stay out of sight for more than another three or four days. And the wine selection—rotgut! But it was the alcohol content that mattered most and this was a case of needs must. The Juice's basket was stuffed full of bread, sliced meat, cheese, ready-made sandwiches and cheap muscadine from eastern North Carolina. He decided to take the overflowing basket to Ronnie and fill another basket with provisions. He needed to lie low. When he got to the register and set the basket down, both Rafael and Ronnie were beaming.

Pointing over his shoulder, The Juice said, "I'm...uh...I'm gonna get some more...um...stuff." He looked from one smiling fan to the other.

"I wanna shake your hand," said Rafael. Before The Juice could say 'No,' his driver was pumping his right hand while Ronnie took their picture. The Juice was stupefied. "You don't mind if I take these off?" and before The Juice could speak or react, Rafael had whipped off his sunglasses. As The Juice towered over him, Rafael leaned into his victim's shoulder and smiled while Ronnie clicked away. Then phones were exchanged as Ronnie came around the counter for his turn.

"Man, oh man, Rayette ain't gonna believe this!" As other customers entered the store, they watched the proceedings and mumbled to one another.

"Really, guys, I just need to get a few more things and go—*soon!*"

From the far end of the store, The Juice heard a heated discussion which ended with a man's raised voice, "Yes, he is! Just look at the photograph!" And there followed a woman's excited response, "You're right! *He is!*" Mobile devices started popping out of pockets and handbags and were directed toward The Juice. Even those who weren't sure who this 'celebrity' might be starting taking photos—just in case. Ronnie and Rafael took note of the other people and wore their best smiles as they attempted to be in each shot. They even put their arms around The Juice, who in nearly all circumstances was not a touchy-feely sort. But years of alcohol consumption, as well as recent over-consumption, had rendered his reflexes all but dysfunctional.

As the group of onlookers began to grow, panic set in. The Juice took out a wad of cash, shoved it into Ronnie-the-Nosepicker's hand and growled, "Keep the change!" He then took the basket of food from the countertop, grabbed Rafael by the arm, pleading, "Get me the fuck out of here!"

As Rafael was dragged through the door, he called back to Ronnie, "*Luego*, Dude! Send me your pictures!"

Ronnie's brain cogs made one or two turns, and then the lights came on. He ran to the door shouting, "Hey, man, you can't take the basket! They'll dock my pay!"

Calling out from the car, The Juice replied, "Rafael can return it!" The Juice's door was still hanging open as the taxi sped away.

To each successive customer who came to his cash register, Ronnie put on his best Southern 'shucks y'all attitude' and proudly crowed that he and The Juice were pals.

As the taxi pulled in front of The Juice's apartment building, he was nearly hyperventilating. Rafael had to help the elderly Facebook star—who seemed to have visibly aged in the last thirty minutes—out of the car and into the building. Rafael even carried the basket of groceries. "Hey man, you want that I should help you into your place?" The Juice nodded wearily, and they entered the elevator, The Juice propping himself up on the wall. When they arrived at the right floor, The Juice simply pointed the direction to take. He fished the keys out his pocket and fumbled as he slowly opened the door. The Juice pointed out the kitchen, where Rafael could unload the basket. Being unable to resist, Rafael pulled out his phone and took some pictures. He even peeked around the kitchen door and took one of The Juice slumped on his sofa. *Man, this is so cool!* With the basket emptied, Rafael went to collect his fare. The Juice looked at him with eyes as deep as wells, nodded that he understood, arduously lifted his backside off the sofa enough to reach his wallet, which he tendered to Rafael. Rafael pulled out two ten-dollar bills and said, "This will cover it. I don't need no tip man. This has been great! Um...you gonna be okay?" The Juice just nodded and waved his driver away. The last thing he thought before he fell into what passed for sleep was: *And I wanted Internet notoriety!*

Twelve

The Young Chaplain Apologizes

Jimmy T had postponed his apologies to Rocky and Keys as long as possible. Now it was dinner time. What little courage he had returned to him an hour or so after he left his supervision with Gretchen. In his mind, he was much more masterful than he had been in fact. In his mind, he had refuted all of his supervisor's artful arguments. In his mind he—"You gonna order something?" The young chaplain's musings were interrupted by one of the servers in the dining hall.

"Um—yeah—there's just so much to choose from. Uh, I'll have the roast chicken and vegetables, with extra mashed potatoes, please."

"We fix 'em as you like 'em," smiled the server.

Jimmy took his tray and headed for the table where Rocky was eating. He thought it would be safer to have a table between him and Rocky's quick right fist. And, Jimmy thought, *There would be a host of witnesses this time.* He approached his aggressor with some trepidation. He even felt a throb in his nose. Rocky was chatting with another resident across the table from him and then spotted Jimmy's approach. "You comin' back for a second round, or are you lookin' to upset some more elderly ladies?" Rocky chuckled as he winked at the person opposite.

"Neither one," Jimmy forced a smile. And then, summoning up his best appearance of Christian charity, he announced, "I have come to apologize to you, sir."

"Grab a chair then." Rocky waved at the chair next to the table's other occupant, Stamps—a retired postman. As Jimmy sat down, Rocky added, "But you know, it ain't me you oughta be apologizing to—it's Keys." He asked Stamps, "Ain't she just the sweetest little thing ya ever laid eyes on?" As Stamps had just filled his mouth, he nodded his agreement. While Jimmy was occupied with arranging the dishes and utensils on his tray, Rocky whispered to Stamps, "Watch this!"

As Jimmy lifted his glass to have a drink, Rocky quickly jerked back his right fist as though about to strike. Jimmy jumped, spilling the water across his shirt and trousers. Stamps and Rocky howled. "That was good, wasn't it?" Rocky congratulated himself.

Jimmy's face had quickly shifted from unctuous self-righteousness to grim determination. "Very funny, Mr. Rocky. I hope you're happy."

"Me? I'm always happy. But you don't look so cheerful. S'matter with you, kid?"

"I'm not a kid!" Jimmy barked a little too loudly, as some of the hard of hearing residents turned and looked. Lowering his voice, Jimmy repeated, "I'm not a kid. I'm twenty-four years old."

"Oh, twenty-four," Rocky nodded toward Stamps.

Stamps wiped his mouth with his napkin and turned to Jimmy, looking him up and down. "You're getting up there, kid—I mean chaplain. Watch out or you'll be living here soon!" He and Rocky laughed in the way that only people who have both gotten over themselves and finally become themselves can laugh—no longer taking themselves seriously. Due to his age and upbringing, Jimmy could do nothing *but* take himself seriously. He was God's mouthpiece of both hope and damnation. Serious stuff!

Jimmy was eating more quickly than usual. He wanted to eat, apologize and get out of there. And he still had one more apology to make. "Mr. Rocky—"

"It's just Rocky. Call me Rocky."

"Okay, Rocky. I came here today to say how sorry I am about the misunderstanding last Sunday morning—" Rocky interrupted again.

"Misunderstanding? Whaddaya mean? You reduced Keys to tears. What's there to misunderstand?" He began drumming his fingers on the table. Inwardly Jimmy was cursing himself with the words which had prompted his mother to wash his mouth out with soap when he used them as a teenager. This conversation, too, was not going as he had planned. Both Rocky and Stamps were waiting for him to respond.

Jimmy washed down the last mouthful of food with a drink of water. "I'm sorry, okay? Let's just leave it at that." He stood and proffered his hand. Rocky looked at it for a moment and turned to Stamps.

"I dunno, whaddaya think, Stamps?"

"I say give the kid—I mean chaplain—a break."

Rocky took Jimmy's hand and said, "Apology accepted."

"And now I need to go and apologize to Keys." Looking around the dining hall, Jimmy said, "She doesn't seem to be here."

"Nah," answered Rocky. "She doesn't often eat supper." Then, turning toward the window, Rocky pointed, "She lives right over there. In the garden apartment with the two plants by the sliding glass door. Just go give her a tap. She'll be glad to see ya." Jimmy bade his dining partners farewell and took his tray to the kitchen hatch. He thanked the staff and began making his way to Keys' apartment. He rehearsed in his mind yet another well-prepared speech. Hopefully this would go better than the previous two.

Jimmy was soon at Keys' patio doors, one of which was slightly open. Taking Rocky's advice, Jimmy tapped on the glass. A sweet voice responded from within. "Come hither, my Adonis!" Having no idea who "Adonis" was, Jimmy entered. The autumn sun had faded and the room was lit by several candles. The room into which Jimmy had entered was the living/dining area. He could see the small kitchen through an open hatchway. That left only two doors in the small apartment, only one of which was open—and therein flickered candlelight.

The chaplain coughed to announce his presence, but Keys did not appear. He inched closer to the open door and unimaginatively said, "Ahem."

"I'm hiding," trilled the sweet voice. Jimmy took this simply as a sign of advancing dementia and took the bait. Entering the open doorway Jimmy heard a noise, which was quickly followed by a weighted net falling over him.

"Gotcha, you naughty, naughty boy! Trying to sneak up on me and have your wicked way!" In the darkness, the young chaplain struggled against the cords of the net and fell over. Soon a candle moved through the near darkness and a figure stood over him. It was Keys, and she was dressed in a flimsy nightgown and—as she leaned closer to inspect her prey—Jimmy saw that Keys wore nothing else. To make matters worse, he couldn't help but see that, for a seventy-three-year-old, she still had a desirable figure. As the candle neared Jimmy's face, Keys frowned and said, "You're not my naughty Adonis..." Jimmy's eyes were wide with trepidation. Slowly, our still-supple Keys, septuagenarian extraordinaire, lowered herself and sat on the young man's midriff. She carefully studied her captive for a few moments and then a smile of recognition lit her face. "I remember you! You're that Charlie Chaplin fellow!"

"Ch-chaplain," croaked Jimmy, "I'm th-the um...student chaplain." And then, very weakly, he uttered, "I-I'm Jimmy." He would have proffered his hand had he not been in a net. In Southern parlance, at this point in his predicament, our young Jimmy didn't know whether to shit or go blind. His Baptist upbringing and seminary training had neglected to teach him the etiquette for being netted by a horny older woman when making a pastoral call. (Seminarians beware!)

Too frightened to struggle, Jimmy gulped and gasped, "I uh...I came to um...apologize." Meanwhile, Keys had rested her chin on one hand as she seemed lost in thought. She then seemed to hear his question.

"Apologize? Whatever for?"

"Um...for making you cry on Sunday morning?"

"Unh-huh," Keys said absentmindedly, as her hands began exploring her catch. "My you are young—and relatively firm." Keys sighed, "I remember young—and firm." With that she hiked up her nightgown and whisked it off. "Yes, let's apologize together!"

Now, Dear Reader, if I have built up your expectations of a torrid love scene between Keys and her surrogate Adonis, I must disappoint you and leave that to your imagination. And, if you have read this far, then you undoubtedly have an imagination! Suffice it to say that virginal Jimmy T was about to have an unforgettable evening...for many reasons.

We now hasten to the next turn of events: the arrival of the intended Adonis—you guessed it, Schwanzie! The caped and masked provider of feminine satisfaction had been delayed at his first call of the night, thus providing the window of opportunity for our young chaplain to stumble into Keys' net. When he arrived at Keys' apartment, the patio door was opened wider than usual, but the candles were lit in the normal way. Schwanzie made his entrance, with cape across the lower half of his face. "Where is my delightful little *schiksa*?" No reply. In the same way as Jimmy had done, Schwanzie aimed himself toward the bedroom door, but stopped when he saw Keys' bare, ivory legs lying on the floor. Frightened that one of his flock had expired, he dashed into the room, caught his foot on part of the net and fell face-first across both Keys and Jimmy T. There followed much ugh-ing and oof-ing as bodies tried to free themselves.

"What the—?" cried Jimmy, his upper torso still bound by the net.

"Well, there you are, my Adonis!" cooed Keys. "Look who I caught in my net! The Charlie Chaplin."

"I'm uh, the chaplain—not Charlie," grunted Jimmy, futilely trying to maintain some professional dignity as he tried fruitlessly to tug his trousers up.

"Thank goodness," gasped Schwanzie, as he maneuvered himself off both Jimmy and Keys. "I thought something terrible had happened to you when I saw you lying on the floor." Keys and Schwanzie embraced tenderly and kissed. In a flash, Jimmy had gone from object of passion to 'three's a crowd.'

As Schwanzie and Keys exchanged tender caresses, our young chaplain lay there feeling quite embarrassed. Once more he tried coughing and ahem-ing. Having gained no one's attention, he called out, "Please, can somebody get me outta this net!?"

Thirteen

Of Pygmies and Wine

For a man who always had something to say and always needed to get in the last word, The Juice had now become more reticent, and something of a recluse. Dozens of video clips of his Brucifixion circulated, not only among his family and the community at The Woods, but also all around the surrounding town—not to mention the world. The Juice received invitations to host other wine tastings, largely from fraternities or bachelor parties, with the idea that he would become the outlet for their pent-up frustrations as they too doused him with wine. On the rare occasions he was seen in the grounds of The Woods in daylight, his face had become paler—if that were possible—the pallor of his skin accentuated by his bloodshot eyes. His face was drawn and unshaven; and his eyes had the look of the hunted. Thus, it became a natural pairing for The Juice to pal up with Great White. Thereby the hunted became the hunter, and the Pygmy hunt was on in earnest.

Because The Juice was now more or less in a permanent state of inebriation, his brain was open to the suggestions, fears, and schemes of GW. The administration of The Woods balked at their idea of creating a 'Pygmy blind' from which they could both observe their prey and be protected from the deadly blow-darts. Instead, they had to settle for clumps of trees or large azaleas—with the lids of trash cans for protection. Great White came equipped with his binoculars by day, while The Juice came with a bottle of wine—with two straws protruding out the top. (Why bother with a glass?)

Because The Woods was a special place and not quite like the average retirement community wherein people played golf and bridge, the machinations of GW and The Juice were tolerated within limits. In fact, most of the residents found their Pygmy obsession downright entertaining. On occasion, Keska Saye, Schwanzie and Der Platoniker would hide among the trees at night and bang on toy drums. One would bang and another would reply from another part of the campus. GW and The Juice would grab any passersby and enjoin them to listen, beaming in the confirmation that the Pygmies were real, they were armed, and they were dangerous.

One lazy autumn day, Der Platoniker found a small length of PVC pipe alongside a building that was undergoing renovation. He decided to have a go at turning it into a blowgun and took it to show Schwanzie. Loving the idea, Schwanzie drove them to a nearby Chinese restaurant where they purchased a fistful of chopsticks. The chopsticks were whittled down to make sharp points and then Keska and Twilight wrapped yarn around the darts, providing just the right resistance such that a great puff of air could propel them twenty to thirty yards. Bird feathers helped with the guidance system.

The night arrived when the pranksters had all they needed to bring GW's fear of the dreaded Pygmies to life. The evening was warm and still, with just a hint of summer past. Twilight began to tap on her drum from the balcony of her and Schwanzie's apartment. Keska Saye hid behind an SUV in the nearby parking lot with her answering drum. Schwanzie and Der Platoniker carried a drum, the blowgun and ammunition. The darts had been dipped in a mixture of cayenne pepper and Texas Pete sauce—guaranteed to give the recipient a burning sensation if hit. The Juice and GW were in their usual haunt, mumbling to one another, and straining their eyes to see in the dark. Once Schwanzie and Der Platoniker were in position, the former banged his drum so as to cover the sound of the blowgun. Phewt! There followed a cry of alarm. The dart had found its mark in GW's ample bottom. As The Juice turned to check on his comrade—Phewt!—a dart found its way into his bottle hand, which released his brain-numbing nectar. There followed pathetic cries of "Ouch! It burns! Oh, God, I'm gonna die!" and the like. And the two elderly imbeciles made their lumbering way toward the campus infirmary, nursing their wounds and griping about who had it worse and, most importantly, whether there might be an antidote to the Pygmies' poison.

The nurse in the infirmary listened noncommittally to the woeful tale of the poison dart attack and the danger that lurked on the grounds of their retirement community. Clearly the two men had been struck by darts, but as the nurse studied the darts, she found the use of knitting wool most peculiar for darts meant to have come from Africa. She agreed, however, to have the substance on the darts tested at a local lab and asked that the two casualties remain in the infirmary under observation in the event they had a bad reaction. The nurse took note that The Juice reeked of alcohol and that GW was stone sober. Curious, she mused, smiling inwardly.

Meanwhile, the pranksters had gathered at Schwanzie and Twilight's apartment to raise a glass to their ingenuity. Each took a turn at telling what she or he had seen or heard from their 'Pygmy' attack. Each report was given a 'hear-hear!' followed by a toast. But meanwhile, back at the infirmary, The Juice and Great White were incubating a scheme of their own. Word had got round The Woods about an amusing near *ménage-à-trois* which had occurred earlier in the week. The activities of the three participants mattered not to our intrepid hunters. What had captured their imaginations was the net!

Perhaps they could impress upon Keys their need to borrow it—especially now that they had proof-positive of the threat that hung over all the residents of The Woods. They resolved that—if they survived the night—they would approach Keys first thing the next day.

Fourteen

The Post-Apology Supervision

The week following Jimmy T's initiation into the rites of Venus, he sat in his weekly supervision with Gretchen Beauxreves. He was less loquacious than usual, so Gretchen primed the verbal pump by enquiring about his apologies to Rocky and Keys.

"Um, well...yes...those." Jimmy coughed. "I...uh...think they went pretty well." Jimmy's hands were pressed between his knees and he was slowly rocking back and forth. There was a refrain playing over and over in his head: "I will not tell, I cannot tell!" This, of course, related to his apology with Keys. It is also the case that Jimmy had re-lived said apology scores of times and—God forgive him—he enjoyed it! *Start with Rocky. Spin it out. Try to say very little about Keys!*

"Jimmy? Are you still here?"

"Oh, yessum...I just well...gosh, I have had so much to learn!"

"O-kay," Gretchen nodded, "Try to tell me about it."

"That Rocky is quite a character, ain't—I mean—isn't he?" Gretchen was silent. "I...uh...I mean he's not such a bad guy, after all. And you were right; he does care about the other residents here." He smiled weakly.

"You haven't really told me anything, Jimmy. How did you apologize to Rocky?"

"I met him in the dining hall—for dinner. I had...um...kinda got busy with stuff and before I knew it, hey, it was supper time. So I went there and had dinner with him—and a guy called Stamps."

Jimmy looked to Gretchen, hoping for some indication that he had said enough. No deal. "They both kinda teased me a bit—about being young and all—but that was okay. I apologized, shook his hand, and he even showed me where to find Keys."

"All right, then. So how was the visit with Keys?"

Jimmy's mind was racing. *Don't say too much. Gotta keep cool! Oh, Jesus, help me!* And then he had what seemed to be an answer to prayer: *Skip to the end. Tell her about Schwanzie!*

"You know, Gretchen, these people here have...um...well, they surely have different ways of...uh...going about things." Gretchen simply nodded for Jimmy to continue. "Well...that is...I had made my apology to Keys for making her cry the previous Sunday when... um...this guy came in...wearing a mask and a cape. She called him her 'adontist' or something." Gretchen feigned a cough to cover her smile. Jimmy was starting to sweat and could feel himself blushing. "And well, you know...they...um...started kissing and hugging and all that... and well...I just had to get outta there! It...um...made me feel very uncomfortable." Another weak smile.

"And who was the caped individual?"

"Well...it was Schwanzie—the Jewish guy."

"Does it bother you that he's Jewish?" queried Gretchen.

"Me? No! I mean...well...yes! He's married, isn't he?" Now Jimmy had his trump card.

"I suppose he is. Is it that which bothers you, or the fact that they engaged in physical affection?"

"Maybe *both*!"

"Hmmm, I can see how you might be bothered by the former—but not by the latter. Tell me why that bothers you."

Oh God, she's asking me to think about it! Jimmy was unconsciously sitting on both hands—and still rocking back and forth. "I-I'm not sure why it bothers me...it just does."

"Jimmy, I'm afraid you have to do better than that. Remember, this is your clinical supervision. We're here to explore experiences, thoughts and emotions—especially as they relate to your chaplaincy. No dodging these questions...I'll just keep coming back to them. Let me ask you a question: do you feel that the elderly have no need or desire for physical affection and sex?"

Jimmy shifted in his chair as he struggled to find an answer. "I suppose I did—before I came here—heh-heh," Jimmy was shocked at his laughter.

"And now?"

Try as he might, Jimmy could no longer block his memory. In his mind's eye, Keys was exploring his body, and unfastening his belt... then his trousers and underwear were pulled down, while his arms were still pinned down by the net...But then, Schwanzie appeared in his mental escapade. "Goddamnit!" Jimmy blurted.

"I beg your pardon!" Gretchen straightened up in her chair. "What do you mean by that?"

"Oh gosh, not you, Ms. Beauxreves, it was just him!"

"Him who?"

"Schwanzie." Jimmy gulped. "I was swearing at Schwanzie."

Gretchen made a point of looking around the office. "I don't seem to see him here. Care to explain?"

Jimmy was grinding his right fist into his left palm. "It's...uh... what he *did*! With *her*!" And then it hit Jimmy—he was jealous! He had no sooner lost his virginity to a sweet older woman than he was ousted by a Jewish guy in a cape and mask, for God's sake. *Couldn't he have left her alone for one night?*

"You seem to be taking it all rather personally—" began Gretchen, but Jimmy cut her off.

"You're damn right! The immorality here sucks! What's wrong with the people here?" Jimmy felt as if he were about to burst into tears. *Oh God, what's wrong with me?*

"Well, it might be that moral boundaries that seem fixed at one point in life...well, shift or become blurred later—not for everyone, but certainly for some." Before Gretchen could say more, Jimmy shot out of his chair.

"I can't talk about this anymore right now!" As he donned his coat, he softened his tone, "Please excuse me, Gretchen. Just give me some time. I-I'll be better at next week's supervision." And with that, our confused Southern Baptist chaplain was gone.

Fifteen

The Kids Call In: Keska Saye

"I'm sorry, *Maman*, but it's hard for me to get my head around everything you shared about our father the last time we were here." Alain looked toward his sister, Marie, who nodded in agreement. They had come without the children this time in order to "gain clarity," as they had put it.

"Oh, but there's really nothing else to say about it. Why dig it all up now? How about some tea or coffee?" Both of her children shook their heads. "Scotch or brandy?"

"*Maman*, it's eleven o'clock in the morning!" said Marie.

"Well, you both look as though you could use a drink—perhaps I'll have one? Either of you care to join me?" Keska Saye headed toward her kitchen. Marie turned her gaze to her brother, expecting a negative response.

"Brandy," replied Alain. His sister gave him one of those "Are you crazy?" looks, but Alain just shrugged. *"Maman's* right—I can use a drink!"

Keska breezed back into the room with two brandies, handing one to her son. "Won't you join us?" she implored Marie, but her daughter stood firm.

Taking a sip, Alain asked, *"Maman,* are you quite sure about... well, Dad's infidelities? As we get older, our minds can play tricks on us." He had not wanted to go so far as to mention the 'D' word, *dementia.*

"Dear, sweet Alain, you were always such a sensitive lad. But please don't patronize me. Your father was a cad."

"But *Maman,* what proof did you have?" asked Marie.

"So much for being a 'liberated' woman. Haven't you been supporting victims' rights over issues such as rape and sexual harassment? And here you are insinuating that I am making this up. Really!"

"Maman has a point, Marie."

"Shut up, Alain!"

Alain raised his arms in surrender and let them flop back to his thighs with a loud slap.

"I just want an answer—if you don't mind," Marie continued her inquisition. "Did you have any proof that Papa was unfaithful to you?" Alain slumped back in his arm chair and knocked back the rest of his brandy.

"Oh, I see, my darling daughter. You mean proof like co-eds' panties left in our bedroom? What about a used condom under the bed? At least your Papa was thoughtful that way. Or a bra stuffed behind a seat cushion on the living room sofa—and don't protest, *ma fille,* it was at least a size D. At the time, I believe you were still wearing a B-cup." Marie began to blush. "Oh, your father always liked full-figured women," and with that, Keska proudly lifted her breasts. Now it was Alain's turn to blush.

Her voice suddenly having gone hoarse, Marie croaked, "I think I'd like that drink now."

Keska smiled and turned to Alain, "Another?"

"Why not?"

Keska returned with the two brandies and handed them to her children. Then she lifted her glass and said, "Here's to the truth! Deceit is so tedious." They drank the toast in silence. But Keska's indomitable spirit soon rebounded. "Now tell me about my darling grandchildren!"

Sixteen

The Bottle Runs Dry

It was Great White who had raised the alarm. Having not seen his partner in Pygmy hunting, he had gone around to The Juice's apartment. Not getting a reply, GW went to the administration building and enquired about The Juice with Gretchen. Her first thought was to check The Juice's mailbox, which turned out to be filled with bills and circulars. "And you say he wasn't planning any trips or going away?" Gretchen asked GW.

"Not at all. In fact, he was helping me with something that—if you don't mind my saying—neither the administrative staff nor the grounds-keepers have been willing to assist in."

"Don't tell me...the Pygmy hunt," Gretchen replied dryly.

"The Juice and I were both victims of their blow darts! This is hardly a fantasy!"

"Well, Pygmies aside, I am more concerned about The Juice. Let me go back to my office and retrieve a pass-key." GW dutifully followed her, after which they directed their steps toward the apartment building where The Juice lived. Outside The Juice's door, Gretchen took a deep breath and then knocked. No response. She tried again.

"I've done that," noted a peevish GW.

"It's protocol; this is not a police raid," replied Gretchen flatly. She had had to do this numerous times in her tenure at The Woods. She inserted the pass-key and opened the door, calling The Juice's name as she did so. The sound of voices could be heard—it was the television. The door opened into the sitting/dining area...and certainly The Juice was sitting...*dead*, but sitting. That familiar death-smell of decay and faeces filled the room. His head was bent toward his midriff, in a sort of navel-gazing posture. A wine bottle, with two straws, was still clutched by his left hand. The television control was in his right hand. The light from the television flickered over his inert body in a macabre fashion.

"Oh my God!" GW threw his hand over his mouth.

"I think you had better wait outside," ordered Gretchen. "I'll call the doctor."

Though he was adept at shooting and killing wild animals, GW was in no way accustomed to seeing his own species in death. Perhaps had he mounted a few human heads, he might not have been so squeamish. (In fact, Dear Reader, if native populations were allowed to hunt big game hunters—and make ashtrays and umbrella stands from their remains—it might go a long way toward protecting the wild animal population. It's certainly worth considering. But back to our narrative!)

GW had to prop himself against the wall of the corridor. The odor from The Juice's apartment had followed him, so he took a handkerchief from his back pocket and covered his mouth and nose. His emotions were a mixed bag, but mainly a mixture of shock and bereavement. After all, GW had lost his fellow veteran of a Pygmy attack. Now he alone must remain vigilant for the sake of the entire Woods community. Who would help him prepare the net to trap one of the Pygmies? So many questions arose in the face of The Juice's death. GW decided to return to his apartment as there was nothing more he could do simply standing in the corridor outside The Juice's place. On the way back to his building, Great White stopped everyone he met and informed them of the great tragedy that had befallen The Woods. Most were, in fact, pleasantly surprised that the news wasn't about Pygmies! And The Juice's departure wasn't exactly met with much wailing and gnashing of teeth, only proving the adage that death confers no dignity on those who were assholes in life.

A feature of twenty-first century living is that important news often reaches those most directly affected via social media as the official channels lag behind. And so it was concerning The Juice's departure. His children and grandchildren saw RIP notices attached to videos of The Juice's last wine tasting. Chaplain Jimmy Watkins learned the news from GW as he was walking from the parking lot to his office in the admin building. He did his best to comfort GW, but as he was about to offer a prayer, the latter spied other people who hadn't heard the news and dashed off, leaving Jimmy in mid-sentence. Our young chaplain did his best to take the brush-off in stride and walked on to his office.

Not two hours later, while Jimmy sat at his desk filling in his pastoral calls sheet, Schwanzie, Keska Saye and Der Platoniker appeared at his door. "We're guessing you've heard the news," began Schwanzie. Jimmy felt a twinge of jealousy at the sight of Schwanzie, but quickly chastised himself, putting on his best pastoral countenance.

"Please, won't y'all come in!" He motioned his visitors toward the armchair and settee. "If you mean the news of The Juice's passing, then, yes, I have heard."

"We were wondering whether you'd be willing to take his memorial service?" asked Der Platoniker.

"Won't there be a funeral?"

"Well, no. It seems The Juice was a little too fermented and will need to be cremated," answered Schwanzie.

"Too fermented?" queried Jimmy. "What do you mean?"

"*Alors*, dear Jeemy," began Keska Saye, "Given the average age of residents here, it is not unusual for people to die—particularly shall we say the anti-social types—and for their deaths not to be discovered for several days."

"Oh...oohh...golly, I see! That's terrible. Does...um, *did* he have family here in North Carolina?"

"Not as far as anyone knows," replied Schwanzie, "They are all in the northeast, but even so, he seemed to be alienated from them."

"He kinda rubbed people the wrong way," added Der Platoniker.

Jimmy seemed to be in thought for a moment, and then asked, "Is that why he got the...um... 'Brucifixion' everyone has been talking about—and that I saw in the videos a couple of Sundays ago?"

"Bingo," answered Schwanzie.

"I guess I'll need to talk with Ms. Beauxreves before I can give you an answer..." Jimmy paused, "Because...um...I haven't ever conducted a funeral or a memorial service."

"That's okay, The Juice never attended religious services anyway," shared the ever-practical Schwanzie.

"And we've already spoken with Gretchen," added Der Platoniker. "She thought it would be good experience for you—if you're prepared to do it, that is."

Jimmy was beginning to experience a swell of pride and confidence in his role as chaplain to these seniors. "Well, thank y'all, but just so you know, I'm not ordained yet."

"*Nu?* What's the problem? The Juice wasn't much of a Christian," chirped Schwanzie.

Jimmy tried to let this statement from a Jewish person pass without comment. "Well, what was his denomination—or faith?"

"I would say drunkard," offered Keska Saye. Both Schwanzie and Der Platoniker gave vocal assent while nodding in agreement.

"Heh-heh," laughed Jimmy, assuming this was some kind of joke. "Come on, y'all. He must've had some beliefs." Jimmy smiled expectantly.

"Well, he did believe that no bottle of wine should be left half-empty," said Der Platoniker.

"Or half-full," added Schwanzie. The other two nodded vigorously. "Yes, you could say that he consumed his life to the last drop," summarized Keska.

Jimmy found himself pencilling DRUNKARD on his notepad and underlining it several times. "Well...um...what did he do in life?"

His three guests looked in puzzlement at one another. Der Platoniker rubbed his short beard and then said, "I think I can help." Jimmy sat upright, prepared to make notes. "He treated people as means and not ends. That is to say, other people had no intrinsic value to The Juice—in the Kantian sense."

Jimmy sat blank-faced. "Uh...'Kantian'?"

"Well, he was, of course building upon Platonic, Aristotelian—as well as Augustinian thought...by way of Aquinas, of course."

"Of course...um...excuse me, but what are you trying to say?" asked the befuddled Jimmy.

"Oh, it's quite simple!" piped up Keska Saye. "The Juice was an asshole! I've always loved that American term—it's so expressive."

In his inimitable way, Schwanzie stated, "The guy was a jerk as well as a drunk. Will that do?"

"B-but what am I supposed to say at his service? I can't say what y'all have told me!"

"Oh, why ever not?" coaxed Keska. "It is the truth. So there can't be any harm in it."

"And don't worry, Jimmy. We'll all help with the service—you won't have to do it all. You can call on us to speak during the service," Der Platoniker assured him. The three visitors all rose to leave.

"But y'all! What about hymns or music? Shouldn't there at least be music?"

"Just have a word with Keys—she'll sort you out," Schwanzie replied with more than a hint of irony.

Seventeen

Jimmy Apologizes for His First Apology

Poor Jimmy had wrestled with his conscience since the evening of his apology with Keys. He had tried to expunge the memory from his brain, but to no avail. After all, it was the loss of his virginity...not something most young men or women are keen to forget. (I suspect that you, Dear Reader, have just remembered that experience in your own life. And, hopefully, it was not traumatic. But if so, I make my apologies.) Jimmy's problem was that, in fact, he enjoyed replaying the event—over and over—and especially when he went to bed. It was the sort of memory that interfered with his evening prayers. In fact, it had interfered with just about all of his mental activities since that very night. It had, however, increased the frequency of his nocturnal emissions, as well as those of his waking, hand-controlled variety. And he was agonizing over his ecstasy.

There was only one thing Jimmy could think to do: *I must go see Keys, apologize for what has happened between us and make a clean breast of it. Did I just think "clean breast"...Keys' breasts were clean...and creamy white...mmhh...Oh sweet Jesus, I have to stop this! What's wrong with me? She's old enough to be my mother! Hmmm, but she's nothing like my mother, so that's okay, isn't it? Her body looks at least half her age...well, not that I've seen other women that age in the flesh.* And so continued Jimmy's ramblings through this ethical dilemma. He spent the better part of an hour sitting in his office, following his thoughts through one path in the moral maze, only to find a dead-end from which he then pursued another course. Finally, he picked up his telephone and dialled Keys' number.

"Hello, Keys? This is Jimmy—I mean Chaplain Watkins. I really need to come see you. Would it be possible this afternoon? Come now? Oh, that would be great. Thank you!" Jimmy steeled himself up. *I will pray my way through this!* And with that determination, our young chaplain headed off for Keys' apartment. A few minutes later, he stood outside her door—no entering through the patio door this time! Jimmy took a deep breath and knocked. The door opened and Keys peeped around it, smiling at the chaplain.

"Won't you come in?"

Jimmy stepped inside. The door was quickly closed behind him—and locked. And there stood the woman of his recurrent fantasy in her naughty negligee. "Um...th-thank you, Keys. Let me say uh..." Keys loosened her negligee. "Uh...say from the start, that I...uh...want to apologize—" but he got no further.

Keys spritely jumped on Jimmy, throwing her arms around his neck and her legs around his waist. She kissed him fervently on his mouth and said, "I do so want to apologize with you again, too!" Like an expert equestrian, she guided Jimmy backwards until his calves bumped into the sofa and where they fell, entangled and enraptured with one another. If memory serves, they apologized two or three times that afternoon. (You don't have to take my word, ask them yourself.)

Eighteen

The Kids Call In: Rocky

"So, um, Rocky, sounds like you guys have had some real excitement around here in recent weeks. Maryanne and I have seen some... some uh, really wacky videos coming from here on Facebook—and even YouTube—of a wine tasting that got a little crazy. Um...were you there?"

"Yeah, yeah, I was there, but I didn't video it or nothing. I sat back and watched the fun as the big souse got inundated with crappy vino. I just enjoyed throwing chunks of bread at 'im—you know, like the way, at the fair, you throw baseballs at the target that drops the clown into the water? Except at our shindig, we got to pelt the clown himself! Ha!"

"Sounds like it was a riotous affair, all right, Da—I mean Rocky. How did the clown—I mean the guy—take it? I hope he's okay."

"Oh, yeah, he's fine. He's dead."

"Dead?!" spoke Jason and Maryanne at the same time. "Did it have anything to do with what went on in the videos?"

"Nah." Rocky waved away their concern. "As I said, the guy was a souse. He died of liver failure or something. He drank himself to death. It happens. Say, you two oughta come to the memorial service tomorrow. It should be fun."

"Fun?" Again, husband and wife were in unison.

"That's right, everything is fun here. We got this kid for a chaplain—he's gonna take the service. He's really green, but basically all right. I had to punch him out a few weeks ago, but he was man enough to come around and apologize."

"Dad—uh, I mean Roc—you *hit* him? Shouldn't *you* be apologizing to him?"

"Are you kiddin' me? He had it comin'. He made the pianist cry in the Sunday service, so I give him one—right on the kisser!"

Maryanne cut in, placing her hand on her father-in-law's arm, "Rocky, couldn't you have handled it another, less violent, way?"

Rocky frowned. "I just knocked some sense into the kid. He shouldn'ta shouted at Keys, tellin' her to stop playin' a hymn. Hell, *he'd asked her to play!* When she started cryin', I mighta went a little crazy—but it was just one punch: a straight right." Rocky threw a fake punch at Jason, who jumped back, causing Rocky to guffaw with laughter. "Anyways, everybody's happy now—especially the chaplain. He's gettin' laid by Keys. So ya see, everything has worked out fine." Maryanne jerked her hand away from Rocky's arm as she and Jason stared at each other in disbelief at what they were hearing.

"The chaplain is having sex with this, this *Keys person*—a resident?" Maryanne queried in strident tones.

Rocky looked at Maryanne with pity. "What—you think we're already dead here or in cold storage? This ain't God's waiting room, sweetheart, I'll tell ya! We're all still alive and kickin'—well, apart from The Juice. Whadda you care if one of us has sex?"

"Yes, but you said she is having sex with the young chaplain. Surely that can't be right!"

"Well, why complain to me? Take it up with them—they'll both be at the service tomorrow. See, now ya got a reason to attend! And it's Sunday, anyway."

Maryanne looked primly at Jason. "Well, I think I just might attend." Jason sat like a deer in the headlights, not believing his ears. "Darling? Shall we *both* come?"

"That really wasn't a question, was it?" Jason replied. "All right, yeah, we'll be here. What time?"

"Two-thirty on the nose," Rocky threw another feint at Jason, who nearly fell over—so did Rocky, but from laughter.

Nineteen

From Juice to Dust

Jimmy had struggled for several days to try to put together some semblance of a decorous service for The Juice. He had contacted The Juice's son and daughter (somewhere up in Yankee land)—he couldn't remember where—but both had basically blown him off. The Juice's daughter, Miranda, was more alienated from her father than Bruce Jr. She told Jimmy that if she turned up at the service, it would be to make certain her father was really dead!—and had hung up. Bruce Jr. hemmed and hawed about his busy work schedule and appointments that couldn't be missed. Jimmy tried to squeeze out something about The Juice from his son, but all he got were chuckles about his father getting plastered with wine at his last wine-tasting. "That's probably the only time he got *plastered* that way—if you get my meaning. Hey, you can use that in your eulogy!" And with that titbit, he had hung up.

Jimmy scribbled over several sheets of paper, desperately hoping some inspiration would come. DRUNKARD...father...grandfather...

drunkard...loved wine and gave wine-tastings = drunkard...ass-hole (Jimmy laughed at this one and immediately scratched it out.) *What was it Der Platoniker had said? He treated people as means...* DRUNKARD. "Goddamnit!" Jimmy shouted. "My first memorial service and it has to be for somebody no one liked!" The chaplain cocked an eye heavenwards, just in case the Almighty had taken offense. *Maybe I could fake being sick? Lord, excuse me for cussing a few seconds ago, but I'm having a tough time here. Please couldn't you tell me what to say or do?* It carried on like this right up until the afternoon of the memorial service—and even then, he was still relying on last-minute divine inspiration.

When Jimmy arrived at the auditorium, a small table draped with a white cloth had been placed in front of the podium. In the middle sat the urn containing The Juice's earthly remains. For Jimmy it seemed to mock his puny efforts to summarize the deceased's life. Residents began drifting in, singly and in pairs. Most were chatting in an animated fashion and some were even laughing. Jimmy had attended funerals—and one or two memorial services—but they had been so much more solemn. The young chaplain had worn his best dark suit and a new tie for the occasion, but the residents came in casual dress. And then his heart sank...the four oldsters who were the Card Crew had arrived! He silently cursed and, yes, he peeked heavenwards in the event a slow-motion lightning bolt was headed his way.

It was then that Keys appeared. Jimmy's heart leapt—and not just his heart. She was wearing a smart black number with a plunging neckline. Her cleavage did have the effect of making Jimmy forget that he had neither a eulogy nor a homily. The chaplain walked over to greet his tutor in the arts of love and she threw her arms around him, kissing him on the neck. That warranted a mixture of nines and tens from the Card Crew. She even got lipstick on Jimmy's shirt collar. Murmurs of amusement rippled around the hall. Except for Rocky's daughter-in-law, Maryanne, who was seated beside her husband near the back of the auditorium. She looked at Jason with amazement, but he simply shrugged. As for Jimmy, he smiled nervously and asked Keys to play some songs as the other attendees drifted in. Keys had promised to find out what music The Juice had liked. She received the most help from neighbors who, although they had never been in his apartment, had heard his favourite music belting out from his stereo.

When Jimmy gave her the nod, Keys kicked off with "Harbor Lights"—at which Jimmy turned his head in surprise, but then half of the congregation started humming and singing along. Jimmy smiled weakly and awaited his inspiration. One couple in the back started dancing to the tune. The next song was "Ghost Riders in the Sky," which Jimmy had to admit at least fitted with a memorial service. No one danced, but there were some passable attempts at making the sound of whip cracks—but not, of course, Maryanne, who was looking more aghast at the proceedings. Jason, on the other hand, was beginning to giggle, which annoyed his wife immensely. Young Jimmy found himself moving his arms to the music—as though directing. Next came a couple of The Juice's favorites by the Sons of the Pioneers: "Tumbling Tumbleweeds" and "Empty Saddles." The Card Crew gave the medley an average of seven.

And then, after much fervent praying, the inspiration hit! Jimmy found his voice—but it was that of an AM radio Top 40 host. "Hey, how about that Keys? Is she good or what?" A few people clapped, unused to this side of Jimmy. "C'mon everybody, you can do better than that!" He put two fingers between his lips and let loose a loud whistle. The crowd joined in. Keys got up and took a bow. "Whoa, not too low, little lady! You'll show everything from here to next Tuesday!"

Beside herself with indignation, Maryanne shouted, "You should be ashamed of yourself!"

"I should...but I'm not!" replied Jimmy.

Embarrassed at his wife's outburst, Jason moved over a couple chairs and made body language which said, "She's nothing to do with me."

Jimmy guffawed at the rebuff, and then put his hands to his cheeks and feigned a shocked expression. Keys went back and sat on the piano bench. The numbers crew gave him an average of eight. Undaunted, Maryanne continued, "Call yourself a chaplain?" "Why would he call a chaplain? *He is* the freaking chaplain!" came Schwanzie's retort. "Lady, won't you please sit down!?" His rebuttal was awarded with tens. Those closest to Maryanne urged her to sit down and enjoy the 'show.'

Then Jimmy raised his arms, solemnly, TV-evangelist style, and said, "Let us pray!" Some heads were bowed while the curious simply watched. "Oh God, we are here to remember The Juice. We don't remember much about him, but, hey, that's not our fault. You made him, after all. Am I right, or am I right?" Some of the congregation mumbled their assent; others laughed.

GW shouted, "He was a fine Pygmy hunter! He would have been ready to die to protect you, you unsuspecting—" He stopped and sat down because he didn't know how to finish his sentence. There was a mixed response from the gathered throng. Maryanne leaned over toward Jason, and said, "Pygmy hunters? What the hell is going on in this place?"

"A 'fine Pygmy hunter'," continued Jimmy. "We can't argue with that, can we, God? You made The Juice not only a wine connoisseur *cum* lush," a member of the congregation burped loudly for emphasis, "but also a Pygmy hunter—and he took a blow dart as proof of his bravery. He had a couple of kids, who don't care for him very much— but who are we to judge, eh?" This drew a large number of assents and the odd 'Amen!' Jimmy peeped open an eye at the residents. "Anybody want to add anything to this prayer 'cause I'm about done?" He waited for ten seconds and then said, "Going, going, gone! So 'amen,' Almighty God! And now it's time for some of you to share your thoughts, memories, anecdotes, tall tales—*lies*! Hey, just kidding!" The Card Crew gave Jimmy straight nines.

Schwanzie and Der Platoniker came forward. Schwanzie looked at his fellow Woodsians and spoke. "*Nu?* Most of you know I didn't care much for The Juice...I mean, he was a jerk. Hey, The Juice was a jerk—hah! Kinda catchy ain't it?" As though in agreement, Keys played a few lively bars as Schwanzie made a few quick steps and a twirl. Then, with much ado, Schwanzie produced a rumpled piece of paper and began to read:

> There died a great bore named Bruce
> Who was terribly fond of the juice.
> When St. Peter he passed,
> Received a kick up his ass,
> "For you we ain't got no use!"

There was much applause as Schwanzie received two nines and two tens. Maryanne was nearly apoplectic. She received no moral support from Jason, as he was laughing and clapping harder than any of them. Maryanne, full of moral certitude, leapt to her feet. "Haven't you people any consideration for the dead?" The congregation looked at one another, shrugging and looking bemused. Feeling that she had taken the high ground, Maryanne looked around at any who dared meet her gaze and, with authority, asked again in measured tones, "Haven't you any consideration for the dead?"

"Yes, we have consideration," piped up Schwanzie, "We consider them *dead!*" the crowd applauded and the Card Crew awarded him straight tens.

"Well, I for one, have had enough of this...this..." and then, as with GW, Maryanne had no words, so she turned and left, looking for her husband to accompany her; but he had slid so far down in his seat she couldn't see him. The congregation gave her departure a standing ovation. She stood outside the rear doors fuming and waiting for her husband.

When things were back to as normal as they ever are at The Woods, Schwanzie turned to Der Platoniker, who had waited patiently and with great amusement. "And now to my esteemed colleague."

"I'd just like to say that The Juice did give Schwanzie and me a reason to write limericks. And I guess, well...that's probably the only reason we'll miss him." He too produced a sheet of paper and read:

> Although he had wanted a wife,
> The Juice was but trouble and strife.

He forsook his wife's bed
For a full-bodied red
And married the bottle for life.

The congregation gave the two friends a standing ovation and the Card Crew awarded Der Platoniker the same as Schwanzie.

"Whoa!" shouted Jimmy T, "Looks like we have a tie, folks! You know, I had intended to award The Juice's ashes to whoever wrote the best limerick—'cause nobody else wants them!" He feigned another shocked look. "Tell you what, whoever can make up a limerick on the spot wins the ashes. Sound good?" The congregation gave their verbal support. "Keys, darling, why don't you play some countdown music while our two contestants think?"

Keys gave a little wave and started tickling the ivories. Der Platoniker and Schwanzie each stood in his thinking pose. The tension in the room was palpable. Keys played a medley of game show tunes to heighten the mood. Suddenly a loud voice was heard, and all fell silent:

The Juice was no Aristotle,
When he drank, it was always full-throttle.
He became such a lush
That his brain turned to mush
They poured what was left in a bottle.

It was neither Schwanzie nor Der Platoniker who had spoken, so everyone looked for the new poet among them. It was Jason! Sheepishly, Jason stood and said, "The chaplain told us the ashes would go to *whoever made up a limerick on the spot.*" He shrugged and smiled like a schoolboy.

Schwanzie shouted, "Bravo!" The whole congregation stood and broke into applause. The Card Crew gave Jason straight tens. He beamed at being so appreciated.

Jimmy T called to Jason, "Come on up here and receive the ashes!" Jason made his way forward while receiving claps on the back and congratulations.

Upon reaching the podium, Der Platoniker and Schwanize warmly welcomed him into their limerick fellowship, and Jimmy handed him the urn. In the style of tele-evangelists and game-show hosts, Jimmy leaned over with the microphone and asked. "Whatcha gonna do with 'em?"

Jason looked perplexed at first. He had been so carried away with the proceedings that he had given no thought to what to do with the ashes of someone he had never met. Schwanzie whispered something to Jason, and the latter grinned from ear to ear. "Conga line!" he shouted.

A roar of approval came from the attendees. Jimmy turned to Keys and said, "Hit it, baby!" Jason led the conga line out of the auditorium and onto the grounds of The Woods. Winding their way aimlessly, they looked like a human steam train as Jason was shaking the urn up and down as they congaed hither and thither. And thus were the ashes of The Juice spread on flora and fauna alike at The Woods.

Twenty

Repentance and Penance

Jimmy read the letter of complaint that had been sent to his supervisor, Rev. Dr. Darren Lockwood, at the seminary. He wanted the floor to open and swallow him. The letter was signed by Maryanne Smith. "But that's not all," Darren intoned imperiously. He opened a message on his Smartphone and handed it to Jimmy. "Hit play," commanded his supervisor. Jimmy's spirits sank even further than rock bottom as he watched himself during the limerick session at the memorial service and the conga line that followed.

"How can you account for this...*this* sort of behaviour?" Jimmy remained silent. "Was it your intention to make a fool of yourself and bring our seminary into disrepute?" Silence. "*Was it*?" Darren slapped his hand hard on the desk which sat between him and Jimmy. Jimmy instinctively jerked, but still said nothing. Over the past week, he had asked himself all sorts of questions about that day. He had prayed to Almighty God for his spirit, for words and guidance before the service—and certainly *something* had come upon him! Jimmy even remembered enjoying himself with abandon—maybe the way King David had felt when escorting the ark to Jerusalem. At least Jimmy hadn't stripped his clothes off! Now Jimmy was a bundle of contradictory feelings. His congregation had loved his service! Should he tell this to his supervisor? It was clearly evident in the video. What was he or his supervisor missing? And then there was Keys...

"And what about this *Keys woman*? The letter says she kissed you in a suggestive fashion—" His supervisor stopped speaking to search again through the multipage letter. "Here it is, 'On the neck.' She kissed you on the neck! Jimmy, what's this all about?" And then...inspiration hit again!

"Well sir, she's only about yay high," Jimmy indicated with his hand... "and she's...well, losing it a bit up here," he pointed to his head. "As for the rest, well, sir, it's what they wanted." Jimmy smiled weakly and raised his eyebrows.

"What *they wanted*?" sneered his Baptist superior.

"Yes sir, didn't you see how they suggested the limericks and the conga line? The Woods is well...it's unlike any place I've ever been. The people there are well...*different*."

"Different *how*?" pushed the Rev. Lockwood.

"Well, they...um...they don't act and say things like my grandparents. They're well, kinda like children." Jimmy smiled hopefully—especially as his supervisor had loosened his stiff posture.

Darren sat and thought for a minute—something he rarely did. Maybe the Lord had intervened? "So, you're saying that most of the people at Carolina Woods are demented?"

"*You* said it!" replied Jimmy. He smiled inwardly because he hadn't had to tell a lie.

"My dear, departed father experienced dementia before he died. I have to admit he said and did some very strange things before he died." Jimmy wondered: did he see his supervisor's eyes tearing up. "In fact, everyone in the home where we had to put him—you see, he had become a danger to himself—"

"Of course," Jimmy interjected with real empathy. He offered a silent prayer of thanksgiving.

"I suppose spending eight or ten hours a week in such a place could have its own deleterious effect on you." Darren breathed deeply through his nose and tapped his pencil on his desk. "I admit I was planning disciplinary action for you, young man—perhaps even expulsion from this fine institution. But I've changed my mind." Looking Jimmy in the eye and pointing his pencil for emphasis, "I'm giving you one more chance, as you've been a very promising student until now. I'll keep this letter in my file and we'll say no more about it—as long as nothing like this happens again. Understood?"

"Understood! And thank you, Rev. Lockwood. You won't be sorry, sir! God bless you!"

"Okay, okay," Lockwood shooed Jimmy toward the door. "You just get back over there and do your utmost to clear all of this up. Got it?"

"Yes sir!" Jimmy stood and started to leave the office.

"And Mr. Watkins? Just remember that *they* are the demented souls—not you." Like so many before him who were spared the noose, Jimmy made promises to God and himself about turning a new leaf. From then on, things would be different. But despite his inner protestations, a small quiet voice said to him, "But you are different now."

Twenty-one

Mach Schnell takes Flight

Little had been heard from Mach Schnell after his recital and knock-out by Rocky. He spent even less time making small-talk with fellow residents than before his ignominious night. True to his Woods-name, whatever he had to do in public was done with alacrity: eating in the dining hall, checking his mail box and going for his morning walks. When he did attend any functions, Mach sat in the back row and was among the first to leave. His neo-Prussian pride had indeed suffered long, due to his public disgrace at the hands of a Jew and wanna-be prize fighter.

But that's all right, Mach had mused to himself. He would find another way to get his message across to these unenlightened dupes of left-wing propaganda. Now that there was a president in the White House who clearly supported the social philosophy and racial pride propounded by Mach and others—things would soon be different and Mach would see who was laughing then. Happily, the wall was being built on the southern U.S. border and policies on immigration had been tightened. And Mach continued to develop his network of like-minded individuals and groups across central North Carolina. Truthfully, however, Mach did find it difficult meeting some of the less-educated, tobacco-chewing 'activists' with their 'Make America Great Again' caps. But then, they made good foot soldiers for the greater cause to which they were all committed...and they could be sacrificed.

Mach assiduously avoided KKK rallies and cross-burnings, knowing that such a public association would put off some people in his 'target group'—the upper middle-class—but felt that these were the necessary prelude to the revolution America needed in order to save it from becoming a mongrel nation of witless dark-skinned immigrants. And, truthfully, Mach did feel more than a little ridiculous wearing a white robe and hood. On the whole, he preferred to take his message to the better-educated among white society—both because he felt more comfortable in the company of the upper middle-class and because they were often too comfortable to understand the need for vigilance in the face of a declining white majority. These "sunshine patriots" needed awakening by someone who understood their values, as well the dangers they faced. Mach would be their bellweather.

Yes, Mach had found himself to be a regular *invité* to social gatherings around the local university towns that dotted the central part of the state. He was meeting people of consequence: fellow academics, as well as lawyers, doctors, legislators and business people. He was cheered over the recent months, as more and more confederate flags appeared on private properties. He, and those like him, knew damn well those flags were the more presentable face of the *Hakenkreuz* which had flown so proudly, but for far too short a time, over Germany and Europe in the mid-twentieth century. But its time of resurrection was fast approaching. Mach could feel it! And Mach also knew he must give his fellow residents at The Woods one more chance to board the train of white nationalism or be crushed beneath its wheels.

Mach had learned one lesson clearly from his recital debacle: Don't put yourself needlessly into harm's way! And so, he set himself to making posters and leaflets, which he posted or deposited around the grounds when no one was looking. They read:

Are You Awake?
Do You Know What's Going On?
Come to the Carolina Woods Communal Garden
1:30 pm, December 12th

Mach Schnell's third-floor apartment overlooked the gardens. Like all of the apartments above the ground floor, it had a balcony, from which he would give his definitive speech. He would also be safe from the interference of that little Yiddish gigolo and that maniac, Rocky.

When the day arrived, Mach prepared the balcony by hanging the various flags and banners of America's 'patriots' and white supremacists. He left a conspicuous gap in the middle. Music was playing from within his apartment, recorded by the *Wehrmacht* choir in 1939. As the hands on the clock approached half-past one, Mach peered out to see who and how many had turned up. Both to his dismay and grim pleasure, Schwanzie and Twilight were among the first to arrive. Always a style-setter, Twilight wore a red, lacy bra back-to-front over her sweater. *Well, if the Jews didn't get the message the first time around, perhaps they'll get it this time? Let's see how they feel when their Aryan neighbors begin to wake up.*

When his alarm clock signalled the time to begin, Mach strode onto his balcony like a wooden Mussolini. There were about thirty people gathered in the garden below. The condensation from their breath could be seen rising like a cloud in its infancy. First Mach welcomed them all and thanked them for accepting his invitation. "We didn't know it was from you!" shouted one disgruntled resident.

Before anyone else could speak, Mack unfurled a Nazi flag and let it drop into the gap between the other flags. He then picked up his speech and began. It was a mishmash of Hitler's rally speeches from the 1930s, modern holocaust denials and his own hate-filled ideas. "White people of America, can you not see the bleak future that lies ahead of us if we do not awaken and lay claim to our rightful heritage?" His listeners responded with laughter, insults and Bronx cheers. The Card Crew gave him straight zeroes.

"Great," moaned Schwanzie, "It's more of his Make America Hate Again rhetoric! Our own resident Trump."

But Mach carried on, filled with the mindless passion of his cause! He cared not that half of his audience had turned to leave. But they all stopped when they heard him cry out. Mach sprang into the air and uselessly flailed at the air as he created a comical swan dive in his short journey to the garden path below, where he landed unceremoniously face-first. A number of people clapped. The Card Crew gave Mach an average of nine—an improvement from his last performance. Someone in the crowd said, "That was one helluva dive...I wonder can he do it again, when I have my camera ready?" But Mach was not prepared for a repeat performance.

His audience crowded around him as he groaned in pain. "Was that part of your performance?" asked Twilight innocently.

But all that came from Mach's bloodied lips was, "Mmpherguh," for he had not only broken his neck, but also damaged his frontal lobes.

"What was that he said?" asked one of the residents.

"Probably that he's a Nazi schmuck!" declaimed Rocky, who had recently joined the crowd.

"Then it was probably German," responded Twilight, who then asked Mach to repeat what he had said. The gathered audience leaned downward awaiting Mach's reply.

"Ughmunhfur."

"Definitely not German," stated Der Platoniker. "Anyone else want to try listening?" And being good Woodsians, they took turns listening to Mach's plaintive grunts and groans.

"Well," offered Keska Saye, "I am beginning to feel this is not part of his performance...but it is a fitting conclusion to his deplorable speech." There were many nods and words of approval. "Perhaps I should go report this to Gretchen and Beatrice?"

"Don't rush," Schwanzie called after her.

A few minutes later, Beatrice arrived. A siren could be heard approaching The Woods. The group of residents was still there, stamping their feet and hugging themselves against the cold. While waiting for the paramedics to arrive, Beatrice asked the residents what had happened. Each had the same reply: Mach had put out invitations to come to the gardens after lunch, whereupon he had regaled them with neo-Nazi rubbish and then dived off the balcony. Meanwhile, the paramedics were on the scene and placing a brace on Mach Schnell's much aggrieved neck.

Beatrice looked toward Mach's balcony, still bedecked with Nazi symbols. She shook her head in disgust. "Was anyone seen on the balcony besides Mach?" Everyone had the same answer: Mach was alone.

Gretchen joined Beatrice, who jerked her head toward the balcony. Gretchen nodded in comprehension and went inside the apartment building to remove the flags and banners. As she walked through his apartment, Gretchen noticed that on Mach's desk sat a framed black and white photograph of a man in SS uniform. She made a mental note as she went onto the balcony to gather up the cloth insults to common humanity. Then, going into Mach's kitchen, she found a rubbish bag into which she stuffed the flags. Gretchen felt an involuntary shiver run up her spine.

Back in the garden, the paramedics had gathered what information they needed as to the nature of the injuries sustained by their patient. "It's usually drunk college kids who fall off balconies," one of them remarked to Beatrice. "But we see it all in our work."

As they raised the gurney to place Mach into the ambulance, he gurgled, "Blepherunkguh." And that was the last the residents and staff at The Woods ever heard from him.

~ * ~

In the days and weeks that followed Mach's dive into his final destiny in a nursing care facility, information trickled out regarding his background. Although Mach had protested that both parents had come to the U.S. as refugees from the Nazis, paperwork found in his apartment revealed that Mach's father had been an SS officer who served on the Russian front during the Second World War. He had come to the U.S. under a secret government deal which allowed SS officers, who could provide any information about the Russians—America's new enemy in the emergent Cold War—to come to the U.S. and not face prosecution. Mach's father had also brought his wife, who was an ardent supporter of both Mussolini and Hitler.

In any case, Mach's swan dive was attributed to mental instability leading to attempted suicide. What no photographs or paperwork would ever reveal was that, during Mach Schnell's final harangue, a certain resident had crept into the apartment unnoticed, grabbed Mach by the ankles and tossed him over the railing. Dear Reader, surely you know who it was.

Twenty-two

The Winter of the Great Congregations

The Lord knows—and you as well—that Jimmy T had tried to control his passion for Keys. He really had. He wanted to keep his word to his supervisor, Darren Lockwood, and turn a new leaf at The Woods. Jimmy needed this field placement to be successful, especially as he was halfway through his final year of seminary education. But what an education he was receiving at The Woods! He had expected the retirement community to be something like a warehouse for those on death's doorstep. But these people had blown his preconceptions to pieces with their shenanigans, such as the Brucifixion of The Juice and his wild memorial service (in which Jimmy had played no small part!)...and then there was Keys.

Having arrived at The Woods a virgin and completely untutored in the art of human love-making, Jimmy could never have imagined people in their seventies or eighties desiring—much less enjoying— sex! *I mean, they're old and crinkly*, he had told himself. And then he had found himself caught in a net meant for Schwanzie. Jimmy had even googled the term *schwanz* and was intrigued to learn its slang meaning. Here was a guy who had to be nearly eighty, running around in a cape and mask servicing horny old women. When he had tried to picture his grandparents—or even his parents—engaged in such antics, his mind froze. And yet...and yet these people were *alive*, vital and so uninhibited (he had looked up that word as well, because Gretchen had mentioned it in their supervision meeting).

He had played over in his mind the memorial service for The Juice. What had come over him that afternoon? Was it the Holy Spirit or the Devil? Jimmy couldn't be sure. He remembered a feeling of freedom and exhilaration—something Jimmy was not accustomed to feeling. But from whence had this exhilaration come? He had lain awake at night searching his soul and praying for...for what? Clarity? Understanding? Jimmy had never questioned himself like this. At times, he wondered whether he might be losing his mind. Jimmy's life had heretofore been well mapped out for him: high school, college with Southern Baptist affiliation, Southern Baptist seminary, ordination and then marriage to a nice, young Southern Baptist lady. He and she would discover what they needed to know about sex together—to create children, of course— then Jimmy and his family would serve Baptist churches until he retired or died... whichever came first. And then Jimmy's thoughts would inevitably return to Keys. His mouth would begin to water and his groin stir. Then would come self-chastisement. *Jimmy T. Watkins, get a grip on yourself*—and then *he would*...but down *there*, all the while thinking about Keys.

Jimmy even found himself reading The Song of Songs in the Bible, no longer convinced that it was describing the love of Jesus for his church. "Your stature is like a palm tree and your breasts are like its clusters. I say I shall climb the palm tree and lay hold of its clusters." Now that he had been with Keys, there was no way on earth Jimmy could ever subscribe to that notion of the Bible's love poetry again. *What is happening to me? Will I ever be the same again?*

And: *What if I like being this way?* And indeed, Jimmy did like discovering that he was a sexual being.

But, Dear Reader, for the young chaplain, there was no staying away from Keys. Jimmy or Keys kept thinking of reasons for him to drop by her apartment. After the Christmas Eve carol service—led by a somewhat more sedate Jimmy and an effervescent Keys—she had invited him to come over for mulled wine and a little Christmas present. Jimmy averred that he was not too sure about the wine, but would gratefully accept the gift. Keys had assured him that the mulling process would evaporate most of the alcohol...which was largely true, but she hadn't mentioned the spiced rum which she would add just before serving. She asked Jimmy to wait fifteen minutes before coming over. Jimmy agreed, as he needed to collect the carol booklets and tidy up the auditorium.

When Jimmy arrived at Keys' apartment, he found the door partially open, with a bow on the doorknob. A little handwritten note was stuck to the bow, which said, "Follow me." A ribbon was attached. Jimmy followed the ribbon to the kitchen where it led to Keys, who was presiding over a steaming pot of mulled wine. She was wrapped as a present. The ribbon was taped to another note which said, "Tug here!" Before Jimmy could unwrap his present, Keys put a mug of mulled wine into his hands. "Well done this evening, Chaplain. Here, drink this up. You've earned it!" The chaplain tested the temperature of the spicy liquid and found it just right for quaffing—which he did.

"This is delicious! I've never tasted anything like this before." Keys took his mug and filled it to the brim.

"Once you've enjoyed this, you can enjoy your present!" She skipped merrily away from him into her boudoir. Jimmy's eyes bulged out as he downed the potent liquid in a matter of seconds. He wiped his mouth on his sleeve and set the mug on the kitchen counter, tingling both from the rum and the words that came from the candle-lit room. "Time to tug!"

What was young Jimmy to do? He had tasted the temptations of both Eve and alcohol—and what's more, he was enjoying them. Whatever next, tobacco? Jimmy followed the voice of his septuagenarian seductress and did as he was told, much to the pleasure of both.

~ * ~

January was soon upon the good folks of The Woods and its arrival marked the second semester of Jimmy's final year of seminary. There had been no untoward reports concerning Jimmy sent to his supervisor at the end of the autumn term, thus the chaplain was in high spirits as he began the final four months of his work in the retirement community. With each successive Sunday in the new year, the congregations at Jimmy's services doubled. In his notes for Darren Lockwood—back at the seminary—Jimmy all but crowed about his preaching and the interest the community was taking in his services. He really felt he was getting the hang of preaching to older adults. What Lockwood didn't know was that by then the heat between the community's chaplain and Keys was at Chernobyl levels. *Everyone* knew about them. But somehow the two lovers didn't seem to notice.

The fact that Sunday services were packed was not, as Jimmy hoped, to hear his message of salvation. (Well, a few listened to his messages.) The rest were there to watch the electricity arc over the nearly fifty-year gap between the young chaplain and one of their own. Keys' Sunday outfits became more and more *risqué*, with plunging necklines and pencil skirts with slits up the sides, revealing her colorful garter belt straps. What both amazed and amused the congregations was that Jimmy didn't seem aware of Keys' seductive dress, or—if he did—he didn't mind! The Card Crew were kept busy with the many antics between the two lovers, who fawned all over each other. In fact, they had stopped carrying any cards with numbers under six, such was the entertainment value of their resident burlesque version of the Jim and Tammy Bakker show.

For his part, Jimmy T had dispensed with a tie and had begun wearing open-necked shirts which revealed a gold medallion Keys had given him. Whenever the aspiring minister was particularly pleased with Keys' rendition of a hymn, he had taken to walking over to the piano and kissing Keys on the neck. Jimmy would then turn to his congregation and beam as he exclaimed, "Mmh-mmh! Isn't she delightful—and *delicious!*" Then, as he had done at The Juice's memorial service, he would form his mouth into a perfect O, while placing both hands against his cheeks and feigning embarrassment. The congregation loved it. Keys loved it. Jimmy loved it.

Ironically, Jimmy's services became the picture of ecumenism as Christians of all denominations, as well as Jews, agnostics and atheists came in ever greater numbers. Jimmy's ministerial persona had evolved over the weeks in measure with the swelling numbers. There was now just a dash of the Top 40 radio host, a fair dollop of TV evangelist, a dose of burlesque show MC, and dinner club comedian.

Jimmy's rediscovery of the very human nature of the Song of Songs gave him the idea for a sermon series. For eight weeks in a row, he would preach the eight chapters of Song of Songs. Whenever he came upon a verse which was particularly sensuous, the chaplain would use a variety of faces and/or gesticulations to make his interpretations obvious. There was no drummer to provide a rim shot to underscore Jimmy's remarks, but Keys would use piano chords to the same effect. In week one, Jimmy read, "A bag of myrrh is my beloved to me, lying between my breasts." Looking up at the congregation, he gave a Jimmy Durante imitation, saying, "And what breasts—ha-cha-cha-cha!" Keys shook her generous bosom while running her fingers over the bass notes. The Card Crew held up tens.

Week four saw Jimmy extolling the feminine mammary glands again, "Your breasts are like two fawns, twins of a gazelle, which grazes among the lilies." As he read these words, he cupped his hands and moved them as though stroking a woman's breasts. "Hey, this is in the Bible, folks. I'm not making this up!" Keys would sit at her bench, resting her chin on folded hands, listening to Jimmy and watching him adoringly. His audience loved it.

By week seven, the chaplain and his accompanist were fully involved in the readings. "Your stature is like a palm tree, and your breasts are its clusters." Keys stood as Jimmy, Bible in hand, read the verses, slowly sensuously, while walking around Keys. You could hear a pin drop. "I say 'I shall climb the palm and take hold of its clusters!'" Jimmy's hand reached forth, but remained stationary. The auditorium was hushed, half-expecting Jimmy to act out exactly what the scripture verse was saying. But Jimmy simply turned toward his listeners and winked.

"You big tease!" called out one female resident.

"That's why they call me 'Jimmy T', baby! I tease 'em and I please 'em!" Bass chords from Keys, who was standing over the keyboard while Jimmy's hands traced their way around his lover's outline. Meanwhile, the entire, rapt congregation wildly applauded...well, all but one. It was at that moment that Jimmy noticed the stony face of his field education supervisor sitting in the rear of the auditorium with his arms folded across his chest.

This became one of those moments wherein one knows that there are two clear choices: yield to the demands and expectations of others or step into the wild unknown of one's own existence. Dear Reader, what would you do were you in Jimmy's shoes? But do let us pause here for, you see, I am greatly exercised by the telling. We shall return anon—I promise!

Twenty-three

Hoist With His Own Petard

Great White was now utterly on his own. He alone bore the scars from the now legendary Pygmy attack. No one seemed the least bit interested in replacing The Juice in this important mission. But GW had a plan. The net, which had been used by Keys to capture her regular young lover, was now in GW's possession, and with it he intended to demonstrate once and for all that the Pygmies were indeed real and that they presented a danger to the entire Woods community.

As he sought the most opportune position to place the net, GW's activities began to attract attention from the curious. Several of the retired engineers and physics professors lent their expertise to the enterprise: trip-wire versus spring-loaded trap, counterweight versus load weight of the prey, bent pine tree with trip-wire versus counterweight and pulley system. There was so much to be considered! In the past, of course, GW would simply have shot his prey, but such things were not allowed at The Woods, thus he had to go to all of the bother of building his trap. So be it. As a consequence, Great White was grateful for all the unsolicited help. Some even presented him with drawings of their plans.

Meanwhile, Schwanzie, Der Platoniker, and the other pranksters had continued the occasional drumming—for their own amusement, as well as to keep GW occupied. With winter's short days, and the morning activities at The Woods, followed by the post-lunch siesta, GW's trap-building was limited to the late afternoons before dinner. The dusk provided just enough darkness for the drummers to keep the hunter on his toes. The occasional chopstick dart was fired his way as a ploy to keep his trap-building fervor on the boil. As his collection of darts grew, GW did his best to seek converts to his cause, but to no avail. "Fools," he would say to himself, "don't they realize what's at stake here? That their very lives depend upon the success or failure of my efforts?"

Despite the lack of interest, GW remained undeterred. Having weighed up the options for the trap, GW had settled upon the bent-pine-tree-trip-wire-plan. He did succeed in getting Rocky and a few other fitness fanatics to help rope and pull the tree to the point where it could be tied to a notched stake. Attached to the stake was the trip-wire which ran across the net. The net was covered with the plethora of pine needles lying about the forest floor. Having been prevented from building a permanent Pygmy blind, wherein he could keep lookout for his prey, GW was allowed to erect a camouflage net between two trees, where he could sit, undetected, on his folding camp stool. On these chill evenings, GW brought along a flask of mulled wine or coffee—whichever his mood called for. He knew it was only a matter of time.

And lo, the evening came, when indeed activity was both heard and spotted in the woods! Upon hearing the soft crackle of pine needles underfoot, GW was immediately on the alert. He peered into the inky darkness, vaguely illuminated by shafts of light from the small low-lying footlights along the path. But there was enough light to throw the odd shadow. That was all GW needed. He knew the Pygmies needed to be in striking distance of their victims on the path, but also far enough into the woods to escape detection. And certainly, there was movement in the general vicinity where the trap lay. A small figure darted furtively from tree to tree. *This is it!* GW's heart pounded. His mouth began to dry in the same measure that his palms began to sweat. However, like a wild animal that senses danger, the furtive creature fled the woods for a quick crossing of the footpath. And it was definitely wearing some sort of cloak. GW put the unusual Pygmy attire down to the cold weather in North Carolina this time of year. *Damn!* The figure had disappeared. Great White was determined to wait. *This will be the night!*

The thermos flask was opened and warming sips were imbibed. GW checked the illuminated dial on his watch. It was shortly after eight p.m. The night was young and the hunt was on. GW smiled to himself in smug satisfaction. Soon his catch would put paid to all of his doubters and detractors. Soon the sound of voices attracted the hunter's attention. *Yes! Human targets for the Pygmies!* Except for the height of summer, very few residents of The Woods were out after eight p.m. and most were abed by nine-thirty—especially in winter. But they were the needed bait to draw the Pygmies out for an attack! GW listened hard and searched the night harder still, but the voices came near and then began to recede. *Drat! Nothing!* Great White mused to himself whether he should have put some sort of fruit or meat into the trap. Perhaps these wild people had enhanced olfactory nerves? Then GW realized that he had no idea what Pygmies ate. This was a serious oversight. He would correct it the next time if this night's hunting ended in disappointment. *But wait! What's that?* The small, cloaked figure had returned and had begun his—or her—one never knows with Pygmies—darting about amongst the trees. The problem was this Pygmy seemed to know instinctively where to avoid walking. *The little fellow is playing with me, goddamnit! But not for long!*

Losing his patience, Great White stealthily broke cover and tried his best to creep silently through the woods to get behind the Pygmy.

From there, he would seek to drive the little fellow toward the trap. GW unhooked the flashlight which was attached to his belt. With a little luck, the bright light might temporarily dazzle the Pygmy, thus enabling GW to direct him toward the net. As he drew nearer to his intended mark, the cloaked figure would dash toward another tree. After ten minutes of this activity, GW was becoming well and truly fed up—but he was also disorientated. Now, he had no idea where his camouflage tent was situated, but the sly creature was currently behind a tree only a few yards away. With a sudden dash, GW was certain he could nab the Pygmy. For a few brief moments, neither moved or made a sound. Just as GW summoned up the adrenalin to move faster than he had done for thirty years, the Pygmy made a break first. Luckily for GW, his prey did not run directly away from him, but ran at a right angle across his path of pursuit. Up sprang GW, shouting "A-ha!" as he shone the flashlight into what appeared to be a masked face. But before he could begin to make any sort of identification, GW felt his right foot catch on something, which had the effect of propelling him forward—into his own trap! In one instant, he was scooped up into the net. The force of the pine tree's springing free sent the netted GW bouncing in every direction. He crashed into nearby tree-trunks and branches, before finally coming to rest—with a fierce bump—against the trunk of the pine.

Great White began to whimper, which became a whine, culminating in a crescendo of full-scale weeping. It was as much to do with the shock of being caught in the trap as it was due to the fact that he had soiled himself during the frightful moment. Despite his crying, GW could hear the patter of footfall running away. And so, he wept harder, and would have continued to do so had he not heard the ominous sound of the drums! His adrenal glands were in overdrive. *Good God, I'm Pygmy bait!* GW struggled uselessly against the nylon cords of his self-made trap. And then he heard the crackling sound of approaching footsteps, followed by the ominously distinctive sound of "Phewt!" He soon felt the dart's entry into his backside, after which came the burning, stinging sensation. The drums became louder—to the point that GW did not hear the next puff of the blowgun. "Yow!" This one had struck his upper back. This was followed by another and then another. GW wriggled and screamed until he began to lose consciousness. *He knew this was it.* And the drumming ceased.

Twenty-four

The Day of Reckoning

Dear Reader, I dare not keep you in suspense a moment longer over the fate of our young chaplain. Yes, his field work supervisor, the Rev. Dr. Darren Lockwood had attended what became known as 'the last of the great congregations.' For verily, the Rev. Dr. Lockwood was greatly displeased by what he had seen and heard. But first, when we left Jimmy T, he had just spotted his supervisor in the congregation. It's amazing, isn't it, how many thoughts, fears and outcomes can fly through the human mind in a split second? And this our young Jimmy experienced—along with the classic instincts of fight or flight—in addition to which there was dread of damnation from the Lord Almighty, the shame of expulsion from his Southern Baptist seminary and more—all in that one second!

But Jimmy T did not run! Neither did he behave as a belligerent. Instead, he held up a hand for silence and said in a stage whisper,

"There's danger afoot!" At this point, Keys played the ominous music from *Dragnet*: Bom-pa-bomp-bomp, bom-pa-bomp-bomp-BOM! With ultimate cool that could only have come from above, Jimmy pointed out his supervisor and bade him stand. Not sure what to do, Lockwood slowly rose from his chair. Jimmy introduced him to the residents and then asked, "Dr. Lockwood, are you here to evaluate me?"

Willing to play this absurd scene out for a short while, he tersely replied, "Yes, Mr. Watkins, I am."

"And what do you think of our service so far?"

"I don't think this is the time or place to discuss it. But trust me, I will have feedback for you." With that, Keys played the theme from *Jaws*. The audience showered her with applause. Lockwood looked around with utter disgust.

"Oh, c'mon, Lockie baby. We're all friends here. Are we not children of the same God? Let's hear what you think. *Please?*"

Someone shouted, "Let it rip, Lockie baby!" This was too much for our Southern Baptist minister, for like most of them, he was used to being treated with deference and respect.

"Please try and show a little respect," he responded in a grim and measured tone.

At the pronouncement of 'respect,' several in the congregation ripped into Aretha Franklin's *R-E-S-P-E-C-T*. Keys picked it up and they all sang a few bars.

"Very funny," sneered Lockwood.

"Well, we aren't laughing," shouted Schwanzie.

Having not brought lower numbered cards for weeks, the Card Crew busily began writing zeroes, ones and twos on the back of their cards and hastily held them up. A low rumble passed through the congregation as they showed their judgment to one and all.

Darren Lockwood began to twitch nervously as he searched, fruitlessly, for some retort, some final word to put these crazy oldsters—and this upstart seminarian—in their place. Jimmy T saw his dilemma and again held up his hand. Noting his supervisor's discomfort, he said, "Let me save you the strain." He walked over to Keys, whispered something in her ear and began to walk back to the microphone stand, when he suddenly turned, went back to Keys, pulled her up from her seat and planted a long, wet kiss on her lips while dipping her backwards with a flair. Key's hands fluttered melodramatically in the air and then alighted on her young lover's back. The congregation went crazy. Keys took her seat once more, and Jimmy gave a little salute, grabbed the microphone, gave Keys a nod and they broke into an improvised version of Johnny Paycheck's "You Can Take this Job and Shove It!"

You can take ordination and shove it,
I ain't int'rested no more,
I got me the love of a woman,
You'd probably think's a whore.

There's more life here at The Woods
Than in your seminary's halls,
I've learned y'all are just big hypocrites,
With little tiny balls!

There were hoots and hollers as people got up and started to dance two-steps and whatever they felt moved to do. Lockwood was surrounded by high-spirited Woodsians, several of whom tried to get him to dance. As he struggled to break free of the crowd, Jimmy went for broke in his last verse:

It's true that you don't like a drink
And you don't like to dance.
But damned if you'll be leaving here,
While still wearing your pants!...Go get 'im, ladies!

Needing no other instruction, the residents crowded in on the Rev. Dr. Lockwood, removing first his shoes and then his trousers.

He was left with the minor dignity of his underwear, and some kind soul handed him his shoes as he was slapped on the back and pushed toward the door, embarrassed, but at least not bare-assed. You probably won't find it surprising that he was never again seen at The Woods and, of course, Jimmy T was never again seen at the seminary. I wasn't there, you understand, but I have it on good authority that the aged residents of The Woods actually summoned up enough strength to lift their chaplain and carry him out of the auditorium on outstretched hands, hailing Jimmy as the hero they saw him to be.

Twenty-five

Somewhere...or Other

The Woods had undergone some kind of metamorphosis—and the Pygmies as well. The Woods seemed to be comprised of stainless-steel trees, and the Pygmies...well...they had morphed into a variety of races, shapes and sizes. But they all seemed to be wearing the same costume of olive drab. *Have I fallen through some kind of wormhole?* As he tried to move, the net still had a firm hold on GW. "I'm still alive!"

"The patient is speaking, Doctor."

The Pygmies are speaking English?

"Good evening, Mr...um..." he consulted the patient's sheet, "Mr. White. You've had yourself quite an evening." Again consulting the sheet, he read, "'Caught in a net. Found hanging in a tree at Carolina Woods. Suffering shock and hypothermia. Fought the emergency medical team.' My, you folks certainly have a dramatic life there. Heh-heh. How are you feeling now?"

"What do you want from me?! If you're going to kill me, just get it over with!"

"Whoa, just hold your horses, Mr. White. We're simply trying to help you get over your little...um...mishap. Hospital staff aren't in the business of killing their patients."

"Where's your chief? He said he would get me. Are you the chief?"

"No, I'm the emergency doctor. Don't you know you're in the hospital?"

"Yeah, right. As though Pygmies could even build a hospital." GW started to struggle, but found his arms couldn't move. He began to scream and curse. "Get me outta this net! Please someone!"

"Jesus Christ, now I see why they put the straitjacket on him!" A nurse and an orderly pinned down GW's legs. "Has anyone spoken to his wife? Is this guy totally demented?"

"She's in the waiting area," a nurse nodded her head in the direction. "Want to go ask her, while we give him a sedative—that is, I assume you'll want to give him *something*?"

"Haloperidol—in the backside, as he's restrained. Back in a moment."

As the doctor went out to converse with Choo-choo, the team in the emergency ward unfastened GW's trousers. "Wow!" gasped one of the staff. "Look at this red mark on his rear! Think he's been bitten by something?"

"Or he injects in his ass. We'll need to wait for the tox screen. Let's just get him calmed down."

~ * ~

In the waiting room, the doctor found Ms. G. White—as he assumed was her name—and beckoned her to a quietish corner where they could speak with some confidentiality. "Ms. White—"

"Choo-choo—but you'd probably prefer 'Janet'," she interrupted.

"Um, right, Janet. Has your husband experienced these sorts of...ah, episodes before?"

Janet shrugged, looking quite uninterested—and even bored. She shrugged and said, "He's been obsessed with the idea that there are Pygmies in the grounds of Carolina Woods."

She shook her head in disgust and fiddled in her handbag until she found her cigarettes. Before she could light up, the doctor said, "'Fraid not." Janet rolled her eyes and pursed her lips.

"Pygmies, eh? Well, it seems that he thinks he's been captured by them. Um, has this happened before?" Janet shot the doctor an "Are you serious?" look.

"Can we go outside?"

"Outside? Why?"

"I need a cigarette, that's why!" Janet put the cigarette in her mouth and started toward the door.

The ER doctor followed in her angry wake. Outside, Janet quickly lit up and took a long drag on her cigarette. She folded her arms against the cold and just stared at the doctor.

"Janet, your husband appears to be having some sort of psychotic episode. In fact, he's quite agitated, so I am having him sedated at this very minute. Would you like to see him? It might help to orient him." Janet gave him her most terrifying "You really are kidding, aren't you?" look, took another deep drag and then, surprisingly, blew smoke rings.

Completely perplexed at Janet's nonchalance over her husband's condition, the doctor took another tack. "Look, maybe you don't realize how serious his condition is at the moment, but in any case, you mentioned his obsession with Pygmies. Can you give me some idea how long this has been going on? *Please?*"

Janet sighed theatrically and pulled out her cell phone, flipped through some pictures, and stopped on one particular image. She held the screen toward the doctor. "This was our living room before we moved to The Woods."

"Um...very nice, but what has this to do with your husband's condition?" Janet rolled her eyes again and looked heavenwards.

"Look on the walls—*ALL* of the walls. Animal heads—*everyfuckingwhere!*" Popping her cigarette between her pursed lips, Janet enlarged the photo. "See this?" She pointed toward an elephant's head. "See that? It all started when he killed this elephant for yet another 'trophy' and found himself cursed by some Pygmy chieftain. Now he feels that the curse has come true and there are Pygmies lying in wait for him at Carolina Woods. Who knows? Maybe he's right. In any case, he deserves whatever he gets." She threw down her cigarette and stamped it out.

"And if I may?—the net in which he was found?"

"What do you think? He put it up! Kinda poetic, ain't it? Are we done here? I'm cold and want to go home." And with that, she left.

And the last anyone at The Woods heard of Great White, he was still in a psychiatric unit, maniacally crying out about Pygmies...as well as assaults by various jungle animals—African and Amazonian.

Twenty-six

What Now?

"I've never *not* known what I was going to do next." Jimmy sipped his spiced rum and looked at the many sympathetic faces around the room: Keska Saye, Der Platoniker, Schwanzie and Twilight, Rocky, and of course, his beloved Keys. "I mean, what now? I've quit the seminary and lost my scholarship, so I don't have any income. I'm no longer your chaplain. And...well...I can't go home because my parents are ashamed of me."

"*Ashamed* of you?! Hey, kid, don't worry—you got moxie, and besides, you're now one of us! Right?" Rocky looked around the room at his compatriots, who all gave voice to their assent.

"We won't let you end up on the streets," offered Der Platoniker. "We'll think of something." The entire group sat in silence for a few moments, drinking Keys' superb spiced rum.

All of a sudden, Schwanzie snapped his fingers. "Got it!" Everyone turned their heads in expectation. "It's such a simple solution, it's been staring us in the face!" The group shook their heads. "*Nu?* Marriage!"

"Marriage?" they asked in unison.

"Certainly! *Nu?* Keys and Jimmy love each other, right? So why don't the two of them get married? Problem solved. Am I right?" The room turned quickly into a hubbub of discussion, weighing the considerable merits of Schwanzie's proposition...because they could find no demerits.

Jimmy listened with interest, after which he said, "Well gosh, y'all. It sounds good to me. I'd really like to live here with y'all—I mean, it's like nowhere I've ever been."

"Well, what are you waiting for? She's sitting right beside you." Keska Saye nodded toward Keys. "Ask her!"

The rest of the room took up the chant, "Ask her! Ask her!" Keys sat smiling demurely, with her hands folded on her lap.

Jimmy stood and then knelt decorously before her. "Keys, I can't stop myself from thinking about you." Keys beamed at Jimmy. Keska Saye and Twilight, 'Ah-ed.' "And I can barely keep my hands off you." Keys gave her ample bosom a shake and everyone gave a rowdy cheer. "So...would you marry me?"

Keys threw her arms around the ex-chaplain's neck and kissed him solidly on the lips. Without removing her mouth from Jimmy's, Keys simply gave a hearty thumbs up. "She says, 'yes'!" cried the group. There were hoots, whistles and loud applause.

After an extraordinarily long kiss, the two lovers came up for air. "There's just one thing," said Jimmy. "Where shall we get married and who will do it?"

"I've got it covered," assured Schwanzie. "I have a nephew in Charlotte who's a rabbi in Reform Judaism—he'll marry anybody! Hey, Keys, got any more of this spiced rum? We need to drink a toast!" Keys went into her kitchen and came back with a deep pan and ladle. Everyone passed their cups for refills. Schwanzie bade everyone except Jimmy and Keys to stand. "To the happy couple, *mazel tov!*"

"*Mazel tov!*" echoed around the room. Without a word, Keys slipped over to her piano and began playing "Hava Nagila." Soon they were all dancing with complete abandon—just as you would expect Woodsians to do.

Twenty-seven

The Kid Calls In: Rocky

"S'matter, kid? You don't seem yourself today. And where's that dame of yours?"

"Maryanne's at home." Jason stared blankly into the beer Rocky had poured him. Then he added, "I guess..."

"Whaddaya mean, you 'guess'? Is she or ain't she?"

"Yeah, yeah, she's at home. She said she doesn't want to come here anymore...ev-ever since the memorial service for The Juice. She said she's embarrassed at what this place has done to you...*and to me*...especially my joining in at The Juice's farewell service." Jason took a long drink.

"Embarrassed? At *what*?"

"Um...everything, I guess."

"There you go guessing again, son. Why do you gotta guess when you live with da woman?"

"Ah well...about that. She...uh...threw me out."

"Threw you out? On account of The Juice's memorial service? What kind of kook is she?"

"A bigger kook than I ever realized...Say, you got another beer?" Jason waggled his empty glass.

"I got enough booze to blast the both of us, if you want. How's about a boilermaker? You can crash on the sofa. Fuck Maryanne if she's gonna treat my boy that way."

"Yeah, I would like to have fucked her," Jason mumbled.

"Ha! I knew you weren't getting any. Didn't I tell ya when ya was here before?"

"Yeah, Rocky, you did. And you were right. Sorry I got so pissed off at you."

"Ah, ferget it, son. I just tells things the way they is. I'm sorry for how things've worked out for ya. Really, I am." Rocky went over to where Jason was seated and laid his hand on his son's head. After a few moments, Rocky said, "I just remembered something I gotta do. We'll leave da boilermakers 'til later. Lemme get you annuda beer and I'll be right back. Chill out for a few minutes. Watch a ball game or something...and don't do nothing stupid, okay?"

Jason mumbled, "Okay" and sipped on his second beer.

About fifteen minutes later, Rocky was back. "Grab yer beer and yer coat! We're goin' to a little shindig—in your honor."

"A what in my honor?"

"A shindig, a party. It'll help you forget your problems. C'mon, let's go!" Jason followed his father's directions. Two minutes later, they were in an adjacent building, in the apartment of Keska Saye. Jason recognized a number of the people from The Juice's memorial service: Der Platoniker, Schwanzie, Keys—even the young chaplain was there. He was then introduced to Twilight, a few others and finally, their hostess. As drinks were being served, Schwanzie and Der Platoniker invited Jason to join in their limericks. Keska Saye put on some jazz music and soon the joint was jumping.

Jason was approached by everyone in the soirée, receiving their commiserations over his separation from Maryanne. He gave Rocky a quizzical expression as he received yet another pat on the shoulder. Rocky shrugged and said, "I only had to tell one person."

Rather than feeling resentful that everyone knew about his personal problems, Jason actually felt liberated—and the booze didn't hurt either. Soon Jimmy T and Jason were deep in conversation. Jimmy let it be known he'd thrown in the towel with regard to ordination and he was "shacking up with Keys." Jimmy's eyes lit up as a thought came to him: "Hey, wanna come to my bachelor party?"

Somewhat taken aback, Jason asked incredulously, "Your what?"

"My bachelor party! Keys and I are gonna tie the knot!"

Jason looked from Jimmy to Keys, did the calculation for age differential—but also noted that Keys had a figure that belied her apparent age. He blinked and took another look at Keys, just to make sure it wasn't the beer-goggles effect; but no, she was really attractive.

Jimmy noticed the lengthy gaze and said, "She's hot, isn't she?"

Looking back at Jimmy, Jason agreed. "Yes, she is, and I'd be delighted to attend your bachelor party. When is it?"

"Two weeks from tonight. It should be a hoot."

"Well, judging from what I've seen at The Woods so far, I'm quite sure you're right. Congratulations!"

"Hey—maybe you can lead another conga line, just like you did at the memorial service?!"

Jason laughed at the memory and shrugged. "Who knows? With enough of this," he wiggled his glass, "and the vibes from this group—anything could happen".

"This place really is something, isn't it? I can't believe how my life has changed beyond recognition in six short months...and the funny thing is, I don't care, 'cause it's great!"

As Jason gazed at the smiling, delightfully engaged people around the room, a strange sense of contentment came over him and his worldly worries seemed to melt away. He also sensed, more than felt, a warm presence next to him, followed by an arm sliding around and entwining with his. The arm came with an enticing scent. "You are enjoying yourself, *oui*?" It was, of course, Keska Saye.

Jason was electrified by the warmth of her touch, but looking into her cerulean eyes, he was mesmerized. Jimmy smiled as he recognized all the signs of the exact same transformation he had undergone. He gave Jason a shoulder chuck and said, "Gonna go find Keys."

"*Alors*, you seemed so uptight or stressed when you arrived. Now I think you are perhaps...finding yourself?" Keska Saye released Jason's arm as she moved to face him. She sipped her glass of wine, keeping her gaze fixed on him. As for Jason, the eyes which had fixated his were like cool Alpine lakes beckoning him to dive in on a blistering summer's day. Keska's free hand reached up to the back of Jason's neck. "Yes, your muscles are more relaxed now. This is good. You were so hunched over when you came in. Now you are...how to put it...*more erect?*" And in fact, he was—in both senses of the word.

Jason had not yet spoken a word to Keska, but in fact, he really didn't need to do so. All that needed to be said was communicated through their eyes, which spoke a much more profound language. He took a last sip from his drink and set it on a table. Jason took Keska Saye's glass and did the same. He then placed both hands behind her head, letting his fingers play through her hair as he drew her face close to his. Their kiss took no one by surprise, and neither Jason nor Keska was keen to break it. By ones and twos, the apartment began to empty. As Rocky passed by his son, he gave him a pat on the shoulder. *Mission accomplished*, he smiled to himself.

~ * ~

The late winter sun shone brightly through the bedroom window. As Jason began to stir, he felt someone next to him and detected the scent of her perfume. He began laughing, without knowing why. His laughter became gut-bursting guffaws, which shook the entire bed. Keska Saye stirred, awoke and propped her head on her hand and watched Jason. "*Tu es content?*" she asked.

From somewhere deep in his subconscious, Jason's university French arose, "*Oui, je suis content—très content.*"

"*Bon, je prends un café.*" She gently pushed Jason out of the bed and patted his naked backside. "Please bring it back here." She patted the bed.

Again, without knowing from whence came such urges, Jason began to dance around Keska Saye's bedroom. He made up his own ballet steps, pirouetted, jumped, dipped and slid his way around the bed to where Keska lay. He firmly planted a kiss on her lips and said, in a mock French accent, "I weel bring madame's coffay een a moment." And with that, he skipped like a happy child into the kitchen.

Minutes later, the two lovers were propped up by pillows, enjoying their coffee in bed. "So, is there a minimum age to move into The Woods?"

"Ha! So now you have changed your tune about this place? Rocky had told me how you wished to get him out of here."

"I would say that it's this place that has changed my tune. I don't know what I was thinking before. Maybe I let Maryanne influence me too much...I don't know."

"Well, you don't have to know, do you?"

"I hear that the young chaplain, well...former chaplain, is going to marry Keys and he's living with her now. He's invited me to his bachelor party."

"I hope you will come."

"Will you be going?"

"*Bien sûr.*"

"I wouldn't miss it!"

Keska Saye playfully twisted the hairs on Jason's chest and around his navel, while she nibbled on his shoulder. "Oh, look, you are making a tent again. How charming! Let me just finish my coffee."

Twenty-eight

The Second Interview

'You understand that there is a three-month probationary period for all new staff?"

"Yes, ma'am, I do."

"Have you any questions about the terms or conditions of your post?"

"No ma'am, I'm very happy with them."

"Good, that's good," Beatrice Charon nodded. "There are some perks to working here, such as one free meal a day at the dining hall; you are able to use the pool and exercise suite before or after work; and—should you need it—the infirmary nurse is available at no cost."

"That's great! I hardly know what to say—this is more than I expected!"

"This is also the first time we have hired a resident of Carolina Woods to become a member of staff. We hope it will be a real success story."

"Yes, ma'am, me too."

"When can you start?"

"I'm here—how about now?"

"I was kinda hoping you'd say that," smiled Beatrice, who then added, "I don't think you'll need an orientation tour, will you?"

"No ma'am, that won't be necessary."

Beatrice stood, extended her hand and said, "Welcome to your role as the new social activities director for Carolina Woods. And happily, you will have the same supervisor."

Gretchen Beauxreves arose from her chair as she beamed at Jimmy, refusing his extended hand, but giving him a hug instead. "Congratulations on your marriage to Keys, Jimmy. You're a credit to your gender." Gretchen gave him a wink and a nod.

"Yes, Jimmy, the service was lovely—Jewish cum Christian. It was a treat."

"Well, as Schwanzie likes to say, the Jews had Jesus long before we Christians got hold of him."

Beatrice smiled warmly. "Jimmy, I think you're going to fit in just fine."

"Thanks—both of you—I won't let you down."

"And, that little mustache you've grown—it really works a treat on you."

"So glad you kept your jacket, too! We do apologize for the jokes when you first arrived." Jimmy looked at his red jacket embellished with **Chaplin.** He laughed.

"Well, it only took me five or six months working here—and watching a half-dozen black and white films with Schwanzie and Twilight—to figure it out!" Jimmy turned to leave. "Thanks, y'all...this... this time at The Woods has been the best experience of my life."

"We hope it is just the beginning of a long series of great experiences. Remember, this is where you live your dreams."

"Don't forget your hat and walking stick." Gretchen handed them to Jimmy.

Jimmy donned his bowler hat, twitched his mustache, said "Tootle-pip," and toddled off, happily twirling his walking stick.

~ * ~

Woods and forests are funny things. They hold such power over and within the human psyche. Hansel and Gretel, Snow White, the Big Bad Wolf, Robin Hood, as well as Schwanzie, Great White, and The Juice, all had their adventures in the forest—and in our imaginations. Woods can conceal as well as reveal. There is mystery and beauty. At night, they harbor fear and anxiety for timid humanity, too used to artificial light. In daylight, they beckon us for a welcome stroll. Won't you come in?

Meet Jack N. Lawson

Jack Lawson grew up in North Carolina. As an ordained minister, he worked as a prison chaplain in North Carolina and Ohio, and later served as a parish minister in the U.S. and the United Kingdom. After earning a PhD in Hebrew Bible, he taught both ministerial candidates and lay people in the English counties of Kent and Norfolk. After leaving parish ministry in 1997, Jack worked for the Countryside Agency, focusing on rural economic regeneration and managing a European Social Fund grant between Kent and Nord-Pas-de-Calais. In the process, he developed an intense love of France and the French people. Later, Jack spent more than 12 years as training and development officer for the Methodist Church in East Anglia. Jack is married to Chris, a former mental health specialist, who worked with children and families in the UK. They now reside in Lower Normandy, France.

Other Works From The Pen Of

Jack N. Lawson

No Good Deed - A Vietnam veteran seeks to find peace within himself, first as a circus clown and later as an ordained minister. Events in his church conspire to reignite his PTSD.

Criminal Justice - A prison chaplain uncovers criminal victimization of inmates by the staff and must decide to risk his job/ life for the sake of justice.

Letter to Our Readers

Enjoy this book?

You can make a difference.

As an independent publisher, Wings ePress, Inc. does not have the financial clout of the large New York publishers. We can't afford large magazine spreads or subway posters to tell people about our quality books.

But we do have something much more effective and powerful than ads. We have a large base of loyal readers.

Honest reviews help bring the attention of new readers to our books.

If you enjoyed this book, we would appreciate it if you would spend a few minutes posting a review on the site where you purchased this book or on the Wings ePress, Inc. webpages at: https://wingsepress.com/

Thank You

Visit Our Website

*For The Full Inventory
Of Quality Books:*

*Wings ePress.Inc
https://wingsepress.com/*

*Quality trade paperbacks and downloads
in multiple formats,
in genres ranging from light romantic comedy
to general fiction and horror.
Wings has something for every reader's taste.
Visit the website, then bookmark it.*
We add new titles each month!

Wings ePress Inc.
3000 N. Rock Road
Newton, KS 67114

Printed in Great Britain
by Amazon

87181081R00095